A CONTEMPORARY ROMANCE NOVEL

Two wrongs
don't mend hearts
like ours.

dangerous hearts

A STOLEN MELODY DUET #1

K.K. Allen

Books
by K.K. Allen

Sweet & Inspirational Contemporary Romance
Up in the Treehouse
Under the Bleachers

Sweet & Sexy Contemporary Romance
Dangerous Hearts
Destined Hearts

Young Adult Fantasy
The Summer Solstice Enchanted
The Equinox
The Descendants

Short Stories and Anthologies
Soaring
Echoes of Winter

Copyright

This book is a work of fiction. Names, characters, places, and incidents either are products of the author's imagination or are used fictitiously. Any resemblance to actual events or locales or persons, living or dead, is coincidental.

Copyright © 2017 by K.K. Allen
Editor: Shauna Ward
Cover Design: Sarah Hansen @Okay Creations
Photographer: Eric David Battershell
Model: Johnny Kane

This book has been rewritten and edited by K.K. Allen.

Original Story and Copyright © 2016 by Mia McAdams
Original Editor: Write Divas **www.WriteDivasEditing.com**

All rights reserved. Except as permitted under the U.S. Copyright Act of 1976, no part of this publication may be reproduced, distributed, or transmitted in any form or by any means, or stored in a database or retrieval system, without the prior written permission of the publisher.

For more information, please contact K.K. at
SayHello@KK-Allen.com

ISBN-13: 978-1546649120
ISBN-10: 1546649123

To all the Schmexy girls out there.

Cinthia,
Wolf is now yours XXOO

dangerous hearts

KA Allen 🖤

#LyricandWolf

Linkin'
Love von Jones
xxoo

[signature]
#Herandoff#

Prologue

Lyric, 15 Years Old

"Lyric, stop!"

My dad's calling after me, but it's too late. I'm already running to my hiding place—a dark corner beneath the stairwell fitted with a single couch. He won't find me here. I fall onto a blue and white checkered cushion, and it releases a hefty poof of dust as a heaving sob bubbles up my throat.

I should have known it would come to this. The last three years have been too perfect. Too … normal. Life is safer on the road, where instability is comfort.

This is what betrayal feels like. Like someone's just thrown my heart in the blender and set it on a slow grind. My daddy has mutilated my heart.

And I, apparently, watch too many horror films.

Suddenly, an unfamiliar voice breaks through my thoughts.

"Are you okay?"

I jump and swivel to find the source of the strange voice, but there's an echo and I'm not sure where to look. My heart rate spikes and my nails dig into the ratty seat that once provided so much comfort.

"Up here!" the voice calls. It sounds like it belongs to a teenage boy.

I look up. The outline of a face peers back at me between the stairs. Someone is there. Watching me. Listening to me.

I should be scared.

"W-what are you doing?" I call out, hoping it's anger he hears over the rattling in my chest. "No one is allowed back here."

The boy chuckles. "Well, then you know why. I'm a rebel. And so are you."

I'm not sure how he managed to sneak backstage. Security at the Aragon is tighter than most venues I've been to. And at just fifteen years old, I've been to most of them.

"Are you here for the show?" I ask, cringing. Why else would he be here?

"Not really. You?"

"Not really," I mimic his nonchalance. Of course I'm here for the show. I'm *always* here for the shows. I practically live here, but that's none of his business.

"If you're done crying, you can come with me."

I glare into the darkness. *Rude.* And a little bit creepy, honestly. He may have piqued my interest, but I won't hide my distrust. "Where are you going?"

"It's a surprise. Come up here and I'll show you."

Isn't that what serial murderers say before they lock their victims up and torture them slowly? My heart is pounding. It should be fear beating itself out of me, screaming for me to run and find my dad. But it's something else.

Something dangerous.

"Who are you?"

"I'm someone who is about to blow your mind and make you forget whatever it was you were just crying about. I already have, haven't I?"

There's a tug at the corner of my lips. His arrogance is both distasteful and amusing.

I push away from the couch and walk slowly to the stairs. The boy is there, still blanketed in darkness, but a dim light from above illuminates his face. He appears to be about my age. And he's smiling. Or maybe smirking—I can't tell. His eyes are kind, and his posture reveals a natural confidence that's almost calming.

There's something about his expression too—something that reminds me of ... me. Not even the dark can conceal the loneliness behind his rough edges. Maybe even some anger. Or maybe it's his dark brown hair, styled into a fauxhawk, that gives him an edge. Whatever it is tugs at my curiosity.

"Well," I say to him with an exaggerated shrug and a step forward. "What's this surprise?"

He extends a hand, never lifting his eyes from mine. When I fail to accept it right away, he raises a brow as a challenge.

I look down and stare at his offering, conflicted. This is beyond strange, and so unlike me to even consider his offer. But I also feel the wave of excitement roll through me, drowning out all reason—and because of that incorrigible rush of adrenaline, I place my hand in his.

He turns and leads me up the stairs to the roof, and when we reach the top, he opens the door with a rusty metal key. Sounds of the city blast us as he steps outside first, propping the door open with his back and letting me slip past him. Adrenaline surges through me, pushing me forward, overriding every alarm screaming in my subconscious.

"How did you get that?" I gesture to the key in his hand, unsure if he can hear the shakiness in my voice beneath the blare of nighttime traffic.

"I stole it."

At least he's honest.

He's still holding my hand when the door slams behind us. I jump again, warming immediately when I hear his low chuckle.

We step out onto the roof and I see the rest of the space. It's wide and open, not much to it. I start to pause, but the boy continues to pull me toward the edge of the roof. My heart seizes in my chest and I try to plant my heels into the cement. This is as far as I want to go.

He tugs on my hand again. "Come on."

I think my heart just might be pumping hard enough to push its way out my throat. I can't do heights. My feet become heavy, and by the time we're a few feet from the edge, they become anchors tethering me in place. The boy turns to face me, a look of admonishment on his face at my resistance.

And then he sees me. Recognizes my fear. I watch as the rough edges of his features soften once more. He steps closer. When he wraps his arms around me, his warmth shocks me. The boy is caring, and the heart beating against the wall of his dark gray cable-knit sweater is loud. Strong. Good.

I'm shaking in his arms, but it's no longer because we're near the edge of the roof. "Geez, girl. Okay, okay, no pressure."

After a few seconds, my breathing returns to normal, but I don't pull away. I'm too afraid to see how close we are to the edge. As if reading my mind, he pulls me toward the center of the rooftop and releases me. We sit facing each other, the moonlight casting a faint glow on us both.

He eyes me curiously. "Are you afraid of heights?"

I nod as I take in a long pull of air through my nose.

"Okay." He draws the word out, thinking. "Do you want to tell me why you were crying down there?"

For a second, my thoughts collide into each other. I'm unsure of how much I really want to tell him. He's been nice up until this point, but I don't even know him. I do know that he dresses and smells too nice to be a runaway. And for some reason, I can't seem to forget the warmth of his hold.

I swallow. I think I can tell him the truth. He may be the first person I've ever confided in about my parents, but if I'm going to talk to someone about it, why not a stranger? He can judge me all he wants, and I never have to see him again.

"My dad is sending me to live with my mother."

"And you don't like her." It's not a question.

My jaw hardens. "I like it here."

"I don't blame you."

Our eyes travel away from each other, past the exterior wall of the roof and toward the Chicago skyline. In our silence, with the sounds of traffic humming four stories below, a calm washes over me. I'm terrified of what comes next for me. I'm angry that I've been given no choice. But in this moment, I let it all go. Thanks to this strange boy who dragged me to a rooftop to cheer me up.

Everything about him so far has surprised me. He gets it. At least that's how it seems. And now that I'm allowing myself to steal longer glances, I can see that he's cute. Definitely boyfriend material, at least in his looks. Still figuring out the personality, though.

"How did you know you could get up here, anyway? I know the hidden spaces of this place better than anyone, but I've had three years to explore." I narrow my eyes at him—as if that will do anything. He's already lured me up here and become familiar with too many of my weaknesses.

He shrugs. "I pay attention." A grin emerges through his tough expression, exposing a shallow dimple in his cheek. My heart jumps in my chest. "I saw some guy up here earlier today when we arrived, so I knew it was possible, and it didn't take me long to find a spare key."

I can't help it. I laugh, then lean back on my hands, tilting my head at him. "I think I like you."

His raised eyebrow gives him away. He's reading way too much into that. Crap. "No, no," I backpedal. "I just mean you were a little creepy back there. You know, voice in the shadows and all. But you're kind of cool now. And I like your hair."

He grins. "Thanks."

I laugh again, this time nervously. *I like your face, too.*

"How old are you, anyway?" I ask.

"Fifteen. You?"

"Same. You're not from here."

He shrugs. "My mom lives in California, my dad is from here, so it's easier to say I'm from all over. I don't like to claim any one space as home."

I frown because that's exactly how I'd prefer to be. It beats the reality I'm facing now. I'm about to leave a place that I love. The only place I could ever think to call home. And I may have just found someone who understands.

"One day we won't need our parents," he says, cutting into my thoughts. His words are few, but heavy.

"What?"

"If it helps with whatever you're going through right now, just remember that. Remember that one day, you'll be on your own anyway, and there's nothing they can do or say to hurt you. You're living this life for you, not them. Play by their rules now, sure, but only you get to decide where you're going."

He's right, but it doesn't resolve how lost I already feel by the thought of moving and not being with my father. We were happy here. At least, I *was* happy here.

I want to ask the boy why *he's* here. Why he seems angry. Where he lives in California. I have so many questions, but I'm distracted as I track his movements. He slides closer until one of his legs is pressed against mine, his face so close, and all the words become a jumble on the tip of my tongue.

"You're pretty," he says, examining me as if I'm abstract art. His eyes flicker between my eyes and mouth, and oh, how I want to be his muse. Air crackles with an unmistakable energy, and before I can stop it, a fire spreads over me—my skin, paint to his canvas.

His closeness awakens my senses in a way that only sees him, feels him, hears him, smells him...

And just as I wish for a taste, he starts to lean in.

His lips are nearly to mine, so near I think I stop breathing, but just for a second. There's a commotion at the entrance of the roof that startles us apart. Our heads turn toward the sound of rattling of metal against wood ... silence

… a shuffle of feet against cement … and then a bang of a door crashing against the wall.

My dad's voice booms through the air, a hint of panic in his voice. "Pumpkin, are you up here?"

My heart jumps into my throat while my eyes grow wide. "I'm here," I call out in a rush and pull away from the boy. My dad will never understand what I'm doing with a strange boy on a dark roof late in the night. When I should be home packing. Giving the boy one fleeting glance as I stand, I hope my hesitation to leave him is clear. His eyes register curiosity, but nothing else.

My dad calls for me again and I jump. "Coming, Dad."

Tearing my eyes from the boy's with a final apologetic glance, I run. When I round the edge of the wall, I find my dad gripping the open rooftop door. His expression reveals concern and curiosity more than anything else. For that, I'm grateful. My father rarely gets angry, and he never gets angry at me. But I've never given him anything to get angry about. A strange boy luring me to the rooftop at night might bring out a different side to him.

"How did you get up here?"

"Uh … the door was open," I lie, stepping past him to the stairwell. "I just needed some air."

My dad pulls me back and wraps his arms around me, squeezing tight. He's happy I'm safe, and as upset at him as I am, this simple gesture warms my heart. I can't imagine my mother ever showing concern for my well-being. "I'm sorry, pumpkin. I know you're upset, but you can't be up here alone. Go home. Get some sleep. We'll talk about the arrangements in the morning, okay?"

8

The arrangements. My stomach churns, but I nod. I won't let him see me cry. "Okay."

He shuts the door of the roof and we make our way down the steps. As my dad ushers me out of the venue and into a taxi, I look up to the roof one last time. The boy is still there, wearing the same expression I left him with—one I know I'll never forget.

Hope.

I never did get that taste.

Chapter One

Lyric

Yes. My name is Lyric. As in song lyrics. As in the music that was playing during my conception. Because my parents are—*were*—rock stars.

I'm not complaining. I'll take Lyric over any of the other asinine possibilities they came up with back then. One drawback: it's not a name that goes unnoticed. Ever.

I'm known as Lyric Cassidy, daughter of a rock icon and a pop goddess who had a swift affair in the nineties. Although my parents were never married and broke up when I was five, they are still one of the most popular couples to grace the music industry. And let's just say, it makes my passion for the music industry ... complicated.

Let me rephrase that.

My fate in the music industry is sealed. Nothing about that is complicated—and therein lies the problem.

Music is my everything. It's the air I breathe. The beat I walk to. The blood in my veins. It's what lulls me to sleep at night. What carries me through the storms of my life ... like the one that just passed.

Except I'm not a musician myself. Not professionally, anyway. I just want to be surrounded by music, however and whenever possible. But the limelight? Well, that's not for me.

It was always a given I'd fall for a rock star. The bad boy type with the raspy vocals who could make an entire sold-out arena swoon. I fell for one, and then he broke my heart when he fell into bed with my best friend. It shouldn't have been a surprise. It wasn't to anyone else. Unfortunately, at the time, I didn't know the importance of shielding my heart like my life depended on it. I know now.

The affair left me with a gaping hole in my heart, aching to be filled. And so I filled it with music. And then my heart was sealed, wrapped up in a tangle of guitar strings, never to be infiltrated again. Have you ever tried flicking a guitar string? Those fuckers are strong.

My bosses were made aware of my situation before I even told them I wanted a new assignment. They had another job lined up for me—by pure coincidence, I'm sure. The job was mine if I wanted it, they said, and I didn't hesitate for a second. It wasn't until they sent the contract over and I saw who I would be working for that I thought to rescind my acceptance. But in the end, I signed, desperate to leave my mess of a life in Seattle. And just like that, the job was mine.

I've never been on a job interview, though not for a lack of trying. Jobs get offered to me like someone's being paid off. It's possible there *is* a payoff, but I'll probably never know for sure. I wouldn't put it past my mother. Ever since her music career slowed down, she's tried everything to crawl back into my life. As if she knows me at all.

I haven't seen Destiny Lane in years. Spoken to her, yes, but as infrequently as possible. I don't want anything she has to offer. She had her chance to be a mother when it mattered, but her music career always came first. My father, Mitch Cassidy, on the other hand—he's still got it. Still hot in the rock scene. Still touring internationally. Still pressuring me to "use my gifts," as he calls them.

Not going to happen.

Less than an hour ago, my plane landed in San Diego. Now my driver, who introduces himself as Elmer—like the glue—is waiting for me at the curb to take my bags. As I climb in the back of the company's gold Jaguar, I take the glass bottle of water from the cup holder and sip down the refreshing fizzy water before finally relaxing into my seat.

I turn down the folding table and place my cell phone on the leather surface, quickly pairing the Bluetooth and thumbing through my playlist. I set it on shuffle and let the rock tunes fill the empty spaces of the car. There's too much pain in silence. Too many thoughts. Too many disappointments. At least when there's music, I can keep my mind busy memorizing lyrics and melodies and drown out my reality. My memories of when it all went wrong.

Turning to face the window, I let the sights of the palms swaying against a cloudless blue background lift my mood. Roller bladers are flying down sidewalks, boats fill the harbor, and everyone seems to be smiling. I don't blame them. If I had to choose a season to live in forever, spring would be it. When everything is bright and alive. And it's the one time of year people can bask in endless outdoor entertainment without suffering through miserable heat or cold.

Feeling slightly more motivated to take on this new adventure, I face Elmer, who's now turning down Ash Street, officially in Downtown San Diego territory. "Are we headed to the office or the hotel?" I ask. In the flurry of activity since the moment I signed the contract, I've had no time to think straight.

Elmer's eyes flicker to mine in the rearview mirror. He must deal with uppity celebs all day because he looks surprised I'm acknowledging his existence. "The office for your two o'clock, Miss Cassidy."

"Thank you, Elmer."

He nods and his eyes return to the road. I turn back to the window. The always-present flutter of anxiety expands and contracts in my chest, effectively tormenting me. Formalities are not my thing, though I always seem to be surrounded by them. It's the air of my parents that never seems to leave me. Others think they need to treat me delicately, as if I'm precious glass. It's annoying, but I've given up correcting people to salvage whatever is left of my sanity.

We approach the all-brick exterior of Perform Live, the artist management company where I've worked since I was fifteen years old. I started as assistant to the assistant office manager and worked my way up from there. The moment I turned eighteen, the management team sent me to work in their Seattle office. After only a few months, I asked for a road job. I'd always loved the road. It was comfort. And I missed it.

So they started sending me on tours to manage the merch. Handling money came naturally, and I worked closely with the tour managers and road managers for three years before getting my first promotion.

Now I do what they do. And I'm damn good at it.

My new position is road manager for Wolf Chapman, rock's ultimate bad boy and the hottest act out there right now. I've seen his type before. Drugs. Sex. Rock 'n' roll. It's not just a saying. It's a way of life, and it's real.

He won't last. He got too hot too soon, which, in my experience, only means he'll stumble and fall—hard. Chances are he won't get up, at least not back up to the top of the charts where he stands right now. I take this as a challenge. I love a good challenge. I'm just here to do my job, even though everything about Wolf screams for me to run.

Talent.

Sex appeal.

Rocker hair.

Drop dead gorgeous smile.

Body of a seasoned linebacker.

Abs made of steel.

Totally not my type. At least, it shouldn't be. Because all of that comes in one pretty little package labeled "ego." The last thing I need after my embarrassing breakup is to be in the presence of another rock star with a massive hard-on for himself.

But I push all that out of my mind as I walk through the company's main doors and toward the elevator, a familiar feeling of excitement beginning to bubble in my chest.

"Lyric, is that you?" A tan blonde with long legs and a Wolf shirt tucked into her short, red leather skirt enters through the opposite entrance and makes a beeline toward me.

Do I know this chick?

She's inches from my face when it dawns on me. I smirk before throwing my hands out in delight. "Terese! No shit. You work here?" We do the girly thing and squeal, hug, and rock from side to side before letting each other go.

I know Terese from when Tony, my asshole ex, booked a three-month run in the Vegas hotel where she worked. We spent all our free time together because *the ex*, of course, was too busy to spend time with me.

"I do," she says. "Moved from Vegas last August and haven't looked back. Please tell me you'll be in promotions with me. Can you imagine how much fun we'll have?"

I shake my head, still beaming. "Road manager for Wolf."

Her eyes, bright blue and sparkling from the stream of sunlight behind her, widen in surprise. "Oh, now I'm jealous. What I would give to be on that tour bus…" A sigh wafts into the air as she trails off into dreamland.

I roll my eyes quickly so she can't see the annoyance and shrug. "Well, I doubt I'll be on *his* tour bus, but the tour should be fun. We've got a show in San Diego before we leave. You working that one?"

Her face falls. "No. I'm only assigned to small local shows."

"Then you should hang with me. I'm not working it, just getting familiar with the crew."

Terese lights up again. "Count me in. How long until you take off for the tour?"

"Two weeks. I'm joining the team late. All the planning has been done, but I guess the last manager didn't mesh well with Wolf." I snort.

She winks. "I'm sure you won't have that same problem." There's a flicker of something in her expression, and I know she's about to ask the dreaded question. But she

15

surprises me. "I always hated Tony. I'm glad you two broke up. He's an ass for what he did, but it's for the best."

I like Terese a whole lot right now, but I don't have time to respond. The ding of the elevator reminds me I'm headed for a meeting with the rock god himself.

"I need to get going," I say reluctantly. "I'll call you tonight, okay? We can do dinner."

I practically run the few steps to the elevator and smash the button, trying to catch the closing door. *Score.* It reopens and I rush in, stumbling into the nearest figure. My hands reach out to catch my fall—on the chest of one of the elevator's occupants.

"Shit. I'm sorry," I say.

The space is filled with leather jackets, heavy cologne, a faint hint of alcohol … and testosterone. Lots of that.

As I try to steady myself, my eyes land on *him*. All six feet of lean muscle, tan skin, and caramel eyes. Wolf is standing directly in front of me, a smirk on his face as he looks at my hands on his chest. *Jesus.*

Someone in the background mumbles with a foreign accent, "No worries, love," but it doesn't sound sincere and no one else speaks, making the moment even more awkward than it was before.

I remove my hands from Wolf's chest and turn to face the closing door, hoping to hide the heat rushing up my neck. It's strange how the presence of a rock star changes the energy in a room. What was once stale, boring air is now electrified and magnetic. I want to face him again to get a good look at him and attempt to recover from that disastrous first impression.

Spinning toward him, I plant a smile on my face and meet his stare. "Mr. Wolf, I should introduce myself. I'm Lyric Cassidy, road manager for your upcoming tour."

His smirk fades and is replaced by a crease between his eyes. He stands silently. Is this some kind of power move? I've seen Wolf a million times in magazines, on TV, on billboards, and on T-shirts everywhere. Hell, I've spent my life surrounded by rock stars. If this guy thinks he's going to intimidate me, he's wrong. *Very wrong.*

"Nice to meet you ... *Lyric.*" He releases my name with rasp in his voice and a flick of his tongue. My eyes are on his mouth now. Such a beautiful mouth. Slightly parted and lifted at the corners. Just enough for me to know he's enjoying himself.

I steal a glimpse of the tongue that just held my name. It's gliding across his teeth in one slow sweep. As my eyes track the movement, I have to swallow against the roll of my stomach. *Holy hell.*

That's all it takes for me to know I'm in a knee-deep shit pile of trouble.

I look around at the chuckling bystanders, who are obviously amused by our exchange. I'm assuming the entourage surrounding Wolf includes his band and manager. They've surely seen the way women react to their frontman, and they think I'm one of them. I can't wait to prove them wrong.

My eyes move back to the man with the accent. He wears a suit jacket and jeans, ready for business. "You must be Lionel."

His eyes light up with mischief and a hint of annoyance. "You would be correct." His accent is thick. British. Or Australian. I can never tell the difference.

I don't think he's my biggest fan. It doesn't surprise me considering I'm a female in a typically male role. Now I just want to irritate him.

"Should I call you Lion for short? Or are animal names reserved for your boss here?"

I smile at my own joke as laughter erupts from the people all around—except one. Peering back at Wolf curiously, I'm stunned to see a smile slowly forming on his lips.

"He goes by Crawley. No nicknames needed," Wolf says, his tone striking me below the waist and reverberating through me with every syllable.

All right. So the rock god can take a joke. That's good.

By the time we've made it to the top floor, I've concluded that Lionel Crawley, the band's manager, is British, and I've introduced myself to the entire band too. I almost forgot their keyboard player was a girl.

We exit the elevator into the lobby of the executive floor, which hasn't changed much since I was last here. The walls are bright red with orange accents and black trim. The Perform Live logo, 3D against the back wall of the room, screams importance.

We're greeted by the receptionist and guided to the very last room at the end of the hall with a spectacular view of the bay. As everyone takes their seats, I gravitate toward the window, taking it all in. It's funny—open air heights terrify me. But this, standing behind a pane of glass that protects me from the fall… This, I can handle.

I can't wait to get out on the road. It's views like this, and emotion-filled rock tunes like what's streaming in from the conference room speakers, that give me an itch that can only be scratched by the rush of life on the road. Seeing a different city every day, bunking it on the bus until we can't hold out anymore and need a night of hotel room luxury, watching the stage setup, hearing the excitement of the crowd, and driving away from the venue with our veins still pumping with adrenaline.

It's all a beast buzzing inside of me. Energizing me. Driving life through my every aching bone. Beating down the walls of my chest. I'm always craving for more of it all. More sights. More sounds. The rush of the mob, fans crushing each other to get where I am. To get closer to the band.

That crazy adrenaline that comes with being on the road. Yeah, it makes up for the shitty beds and the lack of closet space.

"You stare as if you've never experienced it."

Wolf's husky voice tears through my thoughts and brings me back to the conference room. I jump and look to my right where Wolf approaches without making eye contact, his arm nearly brushing against mine.

I swallow against my throbbing pulse. "What?" I understand his question; my answer is just taking a bit longer to form after the vibrations from his nearness took over my body.

He chuckles. "Have you ever explored the city? I could show you around. Maybe after dinner?"

My head snaps toward him, and I'm ready to unleash. The moment dinner is mentioned, I have a flashback to Tony and how that relationship all started with an innocent dinner and far too much wine. *Hell no.*

Fortunately, I'm prepared with a comeback. I knew this was coming, but I honestly expected it to take a little longer than five minutes. It appears I've underestimated him.

"You and I"—I point my finger first at his chest and then at mine—"are not going to dinner together. There will be no sightseeing trips or accidental drunken encounters. I am your road manager. I coordinate travel, keep your merchandise stocked, coordinate with the venues, manage the books, and keep you organized. Is that clear? Dinner. Is. Not. Happening."

Wolf surprises me by shrugging his shoulders and stepping back. He's laughing, and that only pisses me off more. "Okay, okay." He throws his hands up. "For the record, I wasn't asking you out. You're not my type."

I'll be honest. I didn't expect those words to come out of his mouth. They sting a little since he's obviously talking about my looks. He knows nothing about me.

I'm still blushing as he continues. "Seeing as you're the *road manager*, I thought you'd be joining us." He waves a hand around the room. "All of us."

Luckily, everyone is too engrossed in their own conversations to witness my humiliation. "We're going out for a bite after the meeting, but feel free to sit this one out. And the offer to show you the city was me being nice because we'll be here for two weeks. And correct me if I'm wrong, but I got the impression you're no stranger to enjoying life through a high-rise window. You look like you need some fun."

Well, don't I feel like a complete fool? I narrow my eyes, needing to redeem myself somehow. Wolf will not get the better of me. I open my mouth to respond but he's already backing up, telling me he's over the conversation.

"Forgive me for misreading the situation," he says plainly. But as he walks away, I hear what he says under his breath. "Or for getting it completely right."

Chapter Two

Wolf

Lyric hates musicians. That much is obvious from her eager refusal of my sightseeing offer. But why such hostility?

It's true, my reputation precedes me. That's no reason for her to immediately throw judgment. Not that I'll prove her wrong. In fact, I'll probably prove her right. It's what I do.

Lyric's reaction earlier tells me she's surprised by my disinterest. It's pleasing to know I've already gotten under her skin, but that wouldn't be enough to get her in my bed. Not that I'd go there. I meant what I said. She's not my type. She might look the part—small, curvy frame; long, wavy brown hair; generous tits; perfect ass; plump lips—but the fire in her eyes tells me she's familiar with *guys like me,* and she knows I'm a perfect fit for whatever description she's conjured up in that pretty head of hers. She doesn't have to say it. It was written plainly in her overreactions and assumptions.

It doesn't matter. Lyric and I are morning and night. I'm a sex-driven rocker, and she likes to play the victim of it all. See, I can judge her too.

Still, as much as I hate that she has a preconceived notion of me, she isn't completely off. She's been burned. It's written in the depths of her expression and I've seen it a dozen times before. Lyric Cassidy is a relationship girl. A hopeless romantic. Any man to replace her last will need to prove to her that he's nothing like her ex.

Tony Rain from Salvation Road. I've never liked the guy. It doesn't help that he's spent the last three weeks at the top of the charts—below me, at number two. I let out a laugh, knowing that must drive him fucking nuts. And now his girl is on my tour. Lucky for them both, I'm not the hero type.

This is where I make myself clear and bow out. Lyric is officially off limits. I may not be quite the asshole she's already pegged me for, but I don't do relationships. Or the chase. Women like Lyric seek the chase. They think the chase equals trust. The chase isn't for me. And I really don't care if she trusts me. I don't have that kind of time, and no chick is worth waiting for when there's a line outside my dressing room. A woman tells me no, I move onto another one who says yes. It's as easy as that—but let's face it: women rarely tell me no.

But sightseeing is harmless.

Sort of.

Maybe I should have suggested the trip during the afternoon. That's safer. Heaven knows I don't fuck with the lights on. It's more convenient that way since the women I screw throw themselves all over me the moment I step off the stage. I want the pussy, but I don't care about the faces. They all blur together, anyway.

It's not like I'm proud of it. Sex is an addiction—same as alcohol, drugs, gambling. I don't do drugs and I don't gamble often. I drink with the best of them, but that's not my addiction.

Sex is what I want. What I crave. What I *need*. Especially with the rush of our music filling music halls worldwide, the blinding stage lights shining down, and the desperate screams from the charged up crowd. The heat of a woman wrapped around my cock is the only release that satisfies me.

Bare breasts in my mouth. Smooth skin beneath my fingertips. Making her moan as I fill her with my adrenaline. Pounding. Over and over until my name explodes from her lips like it's the only word she's ever known.

Fuck. Why am I thinking about sex? I'm giving myself a boner in a conference room that's ninety percent dudes.

Because of her. She's glaring at me from across the conference table, still flushed pink from our exchange. Good. Better to put her in her place now than once we're on the road. We may have a luxury ride, but a bus is a bus, and buses are small as shit. No privacy. No room for misunderstandings.

I let the corner of my mouth curl slightly and raise my chin to her in acknowledgement. With a roll of her eyes, she redirects her focus toward my bandmate Derrick, who sits to her right. He introduces himself, offering his hand, and she smiles kindly. Interesting. It's possible she doesn't hate all musicians, but she's clearly pegged me as her enemy. That's fine.

Lyric seems like a tough chick. And when a woman like that gets burned, she loses trust and makes every guy that comes after suffer for it. It happened to my sister. She swore off musicians four years ago, just when I was first making my way up the charts. She got wrapped up in my crowd, loved the rush, but got burned fast by the first asshole that showed her what this life is all about. She's happier now with her real estate agent husband. Settled. How the hell did we turn out so different?

It's probably a good thing Lyric made herself clear. Sooner or later, I would've come on to her. Riddled heart aside, she's hot. I'm especially enamored with those pouty lips of hers... I'd let her wrap those lips around my cock. And with a fiery personality like that, I'm certain she'd know how to handle every inch. Not to mention, we'll be sharing the same tour bus for over three months—more if I keep her on for the next tour. That's nine months of staying away.

Jesus. The more I think about *not* getting inside Lyric, the harder it is to concentrate on what Andrew, our tour manager, is saying. I shift and try to change my focus to whatever he's going on about.

Doug, the tour director who also happens to be Andrew's boss, will be managing things from the office, so it will just be Miss Cassidy and her blaze of fire who accompanies us. I'd like to say with confidence that Lyric was the best fit for the job, but the tour company didn't give me many options this time around, and I can't help but question how she'll handle this gig.

I don't doubt her skills. I checked up on those, and the tour company had nothing but great things to say about her. She seems capable and strong, and it's obvious she knows the business as well as the rest of us. Maybe even better. Fuck, Mitch Cassidy is one of my idols.

But none of that changes the fact that I've never worked with a chick road manager before. Hours are long. She'll be surrounded by dudes, for the most part. There's a lot of male ass to kiss. A lot of schmoozing. And she'll have to deal with Crawley. I'm not sure if Crawley has a thing against female road managers in general or just Lyric, but he's not a fan. Then again, Crawley has a stick up his ass about pretty much everything.

"We've got a local crew handling the San Diego show in a couple weeks," says Andrew. "Lyric, feel free to roam like we already talked about. Follow Doug around. Get to know your merch crew. Hang backstage. Hell, just enjoy the show and have a good time. It will be a long three months before you get a real break."

I can't help but smirk in her direction. Honestly, I'm considering what my wager will be when the guys and I make bets at how long she'll last on the tour. The road isn't for everyone. It's for practically no one, but the rush of the acoustics on stage is worth it for me.

"Where to for dinner, Wolf?" My bandmate Stryder approaches me after the meeting. Stryder's a chill guy, the kind who just goes with the flow, looking for others to make the decisions because he's happy if everyone else is happy.

When I found Stryder six years ago, he was playing backup for some local band in a hole-in-the-wall club. It wasn't hard to spot his talent. Sure, his tangled blond mess of hair might hide the passion in his face when he riffs on stage, but the guy has got the versatility that I never knew I needed. Funny enough, he was the hardest one to convince to join the band. He was happy with his beach bum lifestyle, surfing his mornings and afternoons away, hitting the rock scene whenever his band would get a gig. But somehow, I convinced him to try something new.

"Prado," I answer automatically. I've been thinking about dinner since we scarfed down fast food burgers and fries at lunch. Food excites me, and there's nothing that pisses me off more than rushing through meals. Prado is the perfect venue for our night. Classy. Chill. Private.

I look over at Crawley and give him the eye. He's been listening, and he's already on it, dialing the restaurant to reserve a room.

Out of the corner of my eye, I see Derrick and Hedge chatting up Lyric. They've got her cornered on the other side of the room, but I can hear everything. Hedge, being the boisterous one of the bunch, is practically begging Lyric to join us for dinner. She laughs at his persistence and turns her head down to her phone before tapping away.

When Lyric slips out the door moments later, Hedge sidles up to me with a grin wide on his face. "Our road manager is hot as fuuuuuck." He groans and I clench my teeth in annoyance. If Hedge thinks he has a chance with Lyric, he's out of his ever-loving mind.

I shake my head and clamp a hand on his shoulder. "She shared a bed with Tony, dude. Leave her be. She's here to work, not play."

Hedge swivels his head and scans my expression dramatically. "What crawled up your dickhole? Lyric's chill; you'll see. She's coming with us to dinner. Bringing a friend of hers." He winks. "Maybe that one's more your type. I call dibs on Lyric."

My chest heats. The last thing this tour needs is drama between our road manager and my bass player. "No way, Hedge. You know the rules."

He throws his head back and laughs. "There are rules now?"

"You know what this tour means for us. We can't afford the drama. You fuck with Lyric and we lose a road manager, then we get screwed halfway through this tour. Don't even think about it."

Hedge huffs and walks away, his iconic golden brown hair bouncing with him—a thick, curly mess that billows three inches from his head.

He may fuck around a lot, but he's a good guy, and he cares about the band as much as any of us. But I'm not stupid. If Lyric gives him an opening, he'll take it. I'll just have to make sure that never happens.

We ride downstairs and exit the building where our black van with tinted windows waits for us beside a gold sedan. I assume that's Lyric's ride since she's already standing there with a cute blonde in a short skirt and a Wolf tee. I smirk. Hedge must be psychic. Maybe I will hit on Lyric's friend. It's usually a good sign when they're wearing my face between their tits.

The band shuffles into the van while Lyric and her friend climb into the Jag. Nice ride. I don't remember the last guy rolling around in an eighty-thousand-dollar ride.

Prado is in Balboa Park, within the walls of the historic House of Hospitality—a beautiful, white, castle-like structure with a private room reserved just for us. Good thing, because tonight is for the crew and close friends only.

We're let off at another curb but I let the guys go on ahead of me while I scroll through my phone. I'm in no hurry, and I've got a call to make.

Rex, my bodyguard—or shadow, as the band and crew call him—sticks with me. He knows how to be present without drawing attention to either of us. Even with his massive build, and mocha skin, he's a gentle giant of a man who only unsheathes his intimidation when necessary. He's also gotten good at reading me. Right now, he assumes I want my privacy and steps out of the vehicle without being asked.

I quickly dial my sister. Lacey lives just an hour from here and I vaguely remember a text from her asking to see me when I got back to town.

"Hey Bay," she answers with a smile in her voice. Bay, short for Beowulf.

"Sis," I say affectionately. "I'm in SD. Do I get to see you?"

"Hell yeah. Just tell me where and when. Bryan is at a conference this week, so I'm free whenever. Please tell me your hotel has a badass pool."

I chuckle. I always did call my sister a fish. "Still with the swimming, huh?"

"A girl's gotta show off her bikini body while she still has it," she says seriously.

I roll my eyes, not wanting to picture my sister in a bikini, or any of the douchebags who I might have to kill when they hit on her. "Okay, pool day it is. I'll call you this week. I'll just be practicing and chilling for the next couple weeks."

"Wow, really? You should stop by the house. You can check out the nursery. Bryan's been painting, and he won't let me anywhere near it. Something about the fumes or some shit. But pool day first. I just bought…"

I listen to my sister talk a mile a minute about bikinis and pregnancy, and by the time we hang up I'm ready for a shot or five. Rex and I make our way through the courtyard and into the private room we reserved just in time for the first cheers of the night.

The room perfectly fits the twenty of us. A long, mahogany dining table stretches across the center of the floor, but everyone is still standing and chatting around the room's periphery. Glass ornamented chandeliers hang from the ceiling, and rock music plays lightly in the background.

A round of shots filled with light brown liquid gets passed around the room. Top shelf shit. It's the only way to party. I toss mine back, welcoming the burn of Johnnie Walker Blue that coats my throat, and am handed another one immediately. My crew knows what I like.

Everyone important seems to be here. My band, some of our crew who happen to be local, and a few close friends from the San Diego music scene. When we blew up four years ago, we tried to keep in touch with everyone. But it seemed the more our music got out there, the less we could trust anyone. Our circle is tight and small, but that's necessary.

I'm the first to sit, choosing a spot on the opposite side of the room, giving me a view of the waterfall in the courtyard and all our guests, including Lyric and her friend. They're outnumbered by a lot. Not my favorite ratio of women to men, if I'm being honest. But this isn't the type of dinner event I want to invite randoms to. Sometimes I just want the intimacy of the familiar, a relief from the constant chaos that surrounds us.

I'm salivating over the menu before I even open it. Not that I need to look. We always order the full menu of appetizers and then plates of entrees to share. But it's so hard to concentrate on food when I find my thoughts competing with Lyric's infectious laugh.

Allowing myself to steal a glance, I see the girls standing with my drummer, Derrick, near the door. Lyric's eyes seem lighter, her posture relaxed. And for a moment, I wonder if I misjudged her. Everything in her demeanor is playful now, her smile a rare kind of beautiful, the complete opposite of how she acted back in that conference room.

She must sense me staring because her eyes dart to mine faster than I'm able to look away. And now I'm frozen. Her paralyzing green eyes hold mine like she's assessing me with a clearer mind than before. Or maybe that's my wishful thinking.

It's too bad she didn't want that sightseeing trip. I wouldn't mind spending a day gazing into those hot-as-fuck eyes while I showed her how many ways I could make her come.

A hand smacks my back, and I know from the force of it who it belongs to. "Jesus, Lorraine. You need to stop with the weight training. You could arm wrestle Rex by now."

"Ha!" she says, sliding into the seat beside me and setting down her beer. "You know I'd beat his ass."

I huff out a laugh. "You know he'd use it as the perfect excuse to toss you over his shoulder just to *stare* at your ass."

She giggles and I smile. Lorraine is as tomboy as they get, but every now and then a dainty girl pops out, and it throws me for a loop. She's got a thing for ripped, baggy denim and male-dominated sports. She watches porn as much as the rest of us and always keeps her dirty blonde hair in a tight ponytail high on her head. But when it comes to me needing advice on women, which doesn't happen often, she's the one I go to.

She may belong to the lickity split club, but she's no stranger to feelings and shit. It's because of her I'm careful who I fuck. I've learned to stay away from the women who carry around all that emotional baggage. And if I ever need a second assessment of any situation, she's always got my back.

"We both know someone else in this room wins the ass contest." She nods across the room, but I ignore the bait.

Lyric does have a fine ass, but I've checked it out plenty already. "Sorry, Lor. She's more likely to suck my dick than pleasure your pussy, and she's pretty fucking set on me being the Antichrist."

Lorraine is mid-sip, and she laughs so hard that beer dribbles from the corner of her mouth.

"Wolf, get your ass over here!" Derrick calls.

Our chat is interrupted as I'm called over to the circle he's formed with Lyric and her friend. I wink at Lorraine, set down my menu, and walk around the table so I'm standing directly in front of Lyric while Derrick introduces me to her friend. Terese, he calls her. I shake her hand and compliment her shirt. It's far nicer than complimenting her rack, which is frankly my favorite part. She giggles, as I knew she would. I grin.

It might be my imagination, but when I look back at Lyric, I swear her eyes darken a little. My lips curl slightly, satisfied, and I allow my attention to wander to the long-stemmed waitress carrying a tray of shots nearby. I hand one to Lyric and then take one for myself, eyeing her with a new challenge. She and I are going to have to get along at some point. Might as well start now.

"To a kick-ass tour and the hotties we've yet to bone!" screams Hedge from the other side of the room. "Sorry ladies." He grins at Lyric and Terese, without sounding apologetic at all. He's holding his drink in the air, waiting for the rest of us to join in.

"Hey," I say to Lyric, and she turns her attention back to me. "To a kick-ass tour."

A hint of a smile appears on her face. "To a kick-ass tour."

Once we've downed our second shot, I take Lyric's glass and hand it back to the waitress.

"Another one!" Hedge screams from the other side of the room. His drunk ass is already on top of the table, so I motion for Rex to pull him down before he fucks up our dinner by getting everyone kicked out. Rex will handle it. He always does.

Hedge is probably the rowdiest of us all and a ladies' man for certain. He's worse than I am, but he's also a kickass bass player, so he can do what he wants—unless it interferes with food.

"I don't know about you all, but I need to get some grub in me before I pass out," I say.

"Good idea," Lyric responds.

If I could put a leash on my eyes to tug them away from Lyric every time they betray me, I would. She doesn't notice me staring at her. If she knew I was unintentionally memorizing every hard and soft line of her features—the soft ones are my favorite—she probably wouldn't be running her eyes up my body.

A rush fills me as she drinks me in. I stifle a laugh and turn away from her probe, deciding not to call her out. I'll just bank that one in the back of my mind for later.

The boisterous chatter continues through appetizers and dinner and into dessert. As hard as I fight it, my focus keeps shifting to Lyric. Her quiet laugh that lights up her face.

Her fearless love for every bite that touches her lips. And how attentive she is with anyone and everyone she's speaking to.

Since when do I pay more attention to someone's behavior than to their body?

I look over and notice Derrick and Terese deep in conversation. The boy is obviously interested, which is nice to see. Out of all of us, I'd say he's the tamest. He's always had his shit together, been kind of the dad of the group. If anyone can reign me in, besides Rex, it's Derrick and his words of wisdom. The boy knows how to give it to me straight when necessary, and it's appreciated. It's probably why he's become my closest friend over the years.

By the time we're ready to leave, we've finished most of the food and all of the overpriced wine, and we're all feeling pretty drunk. The boys want to take the van to the nearest club, but I surprise everyone—myself included—by refusing to join them. I'm going to save the partying for tour. No need to get into any trouble before we even leave town.

Terese hugs Lyric goodbye and takes my spot in the van, curling up next to Derrick in the front bench seat. When they drive off, I'm not oblivious to Lyric standing beside me now. We're the only two left, apart from Rex, who hovers nearby, and Lyric's driver who is opening the back door of the Jag.

There's a warm breeze in the air. It feels good, especially after being stuffed among the other sausages and roasting in our private dining room. But the warmer temperature mixed with the wind causes Lyric to wrap her arms around herself before she nods in my direction.

"You need a lift somewhere, rock star?"

I refused the van ride to the hotel because I just need to breathe for a minute. In fact, I intend on taking the next two weeks to do exactly that. No band, no chicks, no booze. Just … breathing.

So as tempting as Lyric's offer is, I know I should decline. Especially since I've had enough trouble keeping my thoughts of Lyric pure all night. I blame the alcohol, and the fact that I'm fucking horny. It's been a few weeks—a lifetime for my cock. And I'm certain I wouldn't be able to hide my bulge sitting next to her in the backseat of a car. I could probably come just from saying her name again.

Besides, I've got all two hundred and thirty pounds of Rex at the ready. I pull my hoodie over my head and place shades over my eyes. I'm such a cliché.

"Nah, I think I'll go sightseeing. Alone."

She smirks. "Suit yourself." Her eyes dart behind me to Rex. "Looks like you have a companion though." With a wink and a teasing smile, she pinches her tongue between her teeth and slides into the car.

She fucking winked at me. Maybe I *should* hop in her car. Teach her a few lessons on how to handle that tongue of hers. Instead, I contain my grin to just a tug at one corner of my mouth.

As her car pulls away, I cross the street and take the path through the park toward the main road. Rex stays several yards behind me, giving me as much space as possible. He's a good guy. Ex-MMA fighter, always ready to take someone out. Never fucks around with the girls, even though they try. Grunts more than he speaks, but he's completely focused on the job. Protecting me from the crazies. Keeping the paparazzi from getting too close.

We're all staying at the Ritz. It's a thirty-minute walk if I keep a steady pace. I'm in no rush tonight. Time to myself like this is a rare occurrence I cherish when I get it, just not for too long. I can only handle this kind of silence in short sprints.

We wander through Balboa Park, winding through the intricate landscaping and animal-shaped hedges to get to Fifth Avenue. We're only a few blocks from our hotel when Rex clears his throat, signaling he's about to warn me of something.

"Cameras aimed at you at seven o'clock, sir."

Well, shit. There goes my leisurely walk.

It's not like I'm doing anything exciting, but they don't care. Tomorrow morning my leisurely stroll in the park will turn into some fabricated headline news story. WOLF SPOTTED ON DRUG RUN or WOLF CAUGHT HAVING MELTDOWN IN THE PARK. I laugh. The media is good. I'll give them that. I'm hardly as exciting as they write in their articles.

I can see the flashing camera lights now. We pick up the pace. Our strides are longer, steps quicker, until we're only a few blocks from the hotel.

"They're closing in," Rex says, his tone carrying a warning. He's right next to me now.

We start jogging. So do they. I catch one glimpse as we turn a corner. There must be at least five of them. Not so bad. But now they're close enough to start asking questions.

"Wolf, can we have an interview?"

No.

"Happy birthday, Wolf!"

It's not my birthday. At least they didn't bring a fucking cake this time.

I swear these fuckers will do anything to get close. They don't even care what they're capturing, as long as they can make up a story about it. They brought me a cake once to get me to laugh, smile, what-the-fuck ever, because it was when my name was blowing up. They wanted a piece of it all. Now, they don't care what they find me doing. I could be tying my shoe and they'll make it seem like I'm snorting coke.

"Wolf, can we just get one picture?"

I throw them a smile over my shoulder. Every now and then I do what it takes to play nice. But it's not enough for the vultures, always on the lookout for their next meal. I know what they're going to ask if I give them the time they so desperately want, and I don't want to deal with it.

"Wolf, your fans are getting bored of the same songs. Got anything new planned for the tour?"

Heat starts in my chest and radiates outward. They want to wind me up to give them something to write about. *Not going to happen.*

We reach the hotel and Rex stands back, blocking the reporters from coming any closer as I walk into the lobby.

There are several people milling around the entrance, and they all turn to stare at me, the panting dude wearing a hoodie and sunglasses. I must look like a creep. I remove the disguise and head straight for the elevator.

Just as the sliding doors are closing, I reach into the divide to stop them. They retract. I let out a sigh of relief before stepping in, but as I do, my toe catches on the open grooves at my feet. I fall forward, straight into Lyric. Her eyes dart to me with alarm as I propel toward her, catching myself, palms on either side of the mirrored wall she's resting against.

"Well, hello again," I say, unable to hold back my smirk. Maybe I should have let my hands fall onto her chest instead. Payback and all.

I'm breathing quickly, still recovering from my unexpected workout. I catch a glimpse in the mirror of Rex stepping into the elevator behind me, but my focus is on Lyric. I watch, amused, as she straightens her shoulders and looks around me as if I'm not standing right in front of her. If I had a dime for every person who pretended to be unaffected by my presence, I'd be filthy rich—even more than I already am. I chuckle.

Her eyes narrow. "Why are you staring at me?" she says exasperatedly.

Still amused, I turn so that I'm no longer facing her. We're shoulder to shoulder and I'm about to respond, but when a gaggle of teen girls shove their way inside just before the doors close, I change my mind.

"Girls, I'm going to have to ask you to step out," Rex rumbles. He's not a mean guy, but his deep voice is always alarming to those who aren't used to it.

The teens look at him wide-eyed. One looks back at me like she might cry.

"No, Rex. Let them ride. It's okay." I smile, effectively causing them to swoon.

Then the doors close and they immediately start with the squeals. *Shit.*

"It *is* you! Wolf! Oh my God. I love you so much. Can we take a picture with you?"

It's an elevator selfie ride all the way to the twelfth floor, where the girls reluctantly get off. I step out with Lyric on the nineteenth floor, thankful when Rex doesn't follow us down the hall. Still, he watches us, and I know he will until I'm safely in my room.

"Are you following me?" she asks.

This time I roll my eyes. "What makes you think I'm into you?"

Her eyes bulge. "You stared at me all through dinner. You followed me into the elevator..." She trails off when she realizes that's all she's got.

Room 1924 comes into view, so I stop and face her. "You, sweets, need to get over yourself. I haven't hit on you once today. And if I did, you wouldn't be fighting it."

She crosses her arms and glares. "Is that right?"

I step forward and stare directly into her eyes. But Lyric doesn't weaken beneath my gaze. She stands taller. I'm not sure if I like that or not. It's refreshing and infuriating in one tiny, sexy, package.

"Lyric." Her name is so fucking sexy as it rolls off my tongue; I could make out with it. "If I wanted to, I'd have you inside my room and naked in seconds. Don't get me wrong, you're a pretty girl, but where I come from, looking at you during dinner and *you* walking *me* to *my* room is hardly flirting." I wink. "This is me."

She steps backward, seeming startled, and when her back hits the door to my room, I have a vision of her naked flesh pressed against it with me deep inside her. *Fuck.* I know what I'll be getting off to tonight. Her eyes are searching mine inquisitively as the fog lifts from my fantasy. "So I'm really not your type?"

"Not at all," I lie.

She sighs. "Okay, then. That's settled. Nothing to worry about." She pushes off the door and slips past me.

"Nope." I focus on sliding my keycard into the slot.

"That should make this upcoming tour much easier on both of us, then," she says, her voice fading the further away she gets.

My smile never wavers as her footsteps cease, and then I hear her door open and close with a bang. I let out a rush of air at the realization that Lyric Cassidy, after only a few hours, has somehow managed to creep under my skin.

Chapter Three

Lyric

My songbook keeps me company wherever I go—an important lesson I learned years ago after inspiration struck and I realized I'd left it at home. It's like a spontaneous orgasm. An idea can come at any time, and my songbook is my condom, catching my word babies as they fall. I've had this particular book for only a few months now, but that's because I fill them quickly. I have stacks of them in my storage unit back in Seattle.

As my feet soak in the warm pool water and my songbook rests beside me, I'm overcome with inspiration. I knew I would be. San Diego is a beautiful place filled with beautiful people, and I see stories everywhere I'm aching to write.

It's been a few days since I've gone *there*. To that place in the deep, dark part of my mind where emotions and words collide, sparking honesty and vulnerability. My songbook is my private place—*my only place*—to unleash these emotions. Because of that, it's safe to say this is my addiction. My obsession.

A shriek and giggle—*a shriggle*—fills the air, turning my attention to the couple at the other end of the pool. There he is. My new boss, the rock god himself, threatening to toss a cute and entirely too willing victim into the deep end of the pool. My stomach rolls. I don't want to watch, but I'm unable to take my eyes from the scene. Such noncommittal happiness. It's not like they're doing anything inappropriate. He's not even groping her yet, but it's a painful reminder of what I left in Seattle. Tony and Joanna. *Fucking assholes.* Despite their betrayal, I can admit that they happen to be perfect together.

Joanna had been my best and only friend since I moved in with my mom. I asked her to tour with me and even found her a job on the road so she had a good excuse to take a break from college. As it turns out, I am shit at choosing friends. I had been dating Tony for two years when Joanna decided to jump into an affair with him.

To make things worse, I hadn't even considered that Tony would be capable of cheating on me. Bad boy rocker and all, I thought our connection was mutual. We're both cut from the same cloth. Born into the industry. Emotionally detached, but not in ways that make us cold. We're just both able to separate emotion from all the other bullshit going on.

At times, our relationship felt more like a business transaction than anything else. There was a friendship there, and he made my heart beat fast in the beginning, but over time, he only wanted me around when it would look good for him. He got too busy and too big for our relationship. It wasn't about us anymore, it was about the music. But the sex was good. I guess. I've never been the easily stimulated type, but he could still get me to climax some of the time.

Whatever. In the end, he followed his heart—or dick—even though it meant damaging mine. My heart, that is.

I stare across the pool and shake my head as Wolf wraps his arms around the girl's slick body. At least I'm not the only one with issues. That bad boy might just be worse off than I am. At least I've made the decision to abstain from sex until I figure my shit out. Wolf doesn't date. At all. And it sounds like he's perfectly content hopping from one girl to the next. His heart is destructive. Dangerous. The last thing I need. Like Tony. Like Joanna. Fuck all of them.

A tingle races up my spine as an idea strikes. My hands fly to my songbook and the words splatter onto the page. I can barely write fast enough to keep up with the lyrics racing through my mind.

Two wrongs don't mend hearts like ours
Two wrongs can never break our fall
I give, you take, it's no mistake
We're in too deep, losing sleep
Trying to forget what started it all

Angry eyes and a brick wall armor
Lessons learned, paths paved
Shield unyielding, it's a heavy weight
One you'll never penetrate
It's hopeless, no use trying to be saved

You ruined us from the start
Your soul is black, your heart is dark
You tear me up like it's an art
Stay away with your dangerous heart

Can't rely on second chances

Since the first one ripped my heart apart
You're not welcome here anymore
'Cause there's no going back to the start

By the time I'm done, my heart is racing and my palms are sweating. That was probably the most therapeutic thing I've done since the breakup. It feels damn good. I've never written a complete song that fast in my life—not that it's perfect. What first draft is? In my opinion, even final drafts aren't really final. How can they be when every moment of every day, we're learning new things and taking on new adventures? Stories change, just as we do.

I stare at the words on the page in front of me. No matter how healing they may have been, I'm not sure they're words I want to hold on to. Tony was a mistake. One that I don't want to remember. One who doesn't deserve my words. Which is fine. Not every written piece is meant to be saved.

Slowly, I rip the page from my songbook, cringing at the tear line I'm creating. Who knew trashing something so personal would feel so painful. When the page is torn completely, I take a deep breath and walk it over to the nearest trash can, which is already exploding with waste. Without another thought, I add my lyrics to the pile because whatever heartache I feel over Tony is just that—waste.

The quiet night is startling when I finally come out of my songwriting haze. I hadn't noticed Wolf and his lady friend taking off at some point during my writing spell, but the shriggles are gone and I'm alone by the pool. Daylight is fading and my stomach is going crazy with hunger, so I pack my things and head inside. Without bothering to change, I sit at one of the hotel bars to order dinner and a glass of wine.

When the bartender slides my first glass in front of me, I reach for it eagerly.

A throat clears behind me and I freeze, the glass nearly to my mouth. "A pretty woman should never eat or drink alone. I'd offer you company but I wouldn't want your head to grow larger than it already is."

The teasing voice should be grating, but it's familiar and warm, and it *is* nice to not be alone for a moment. Wolf slips onto the stool beside me.

"Ha, ha." I face him with a smirk. My eyes have a mind of their own as they flicker between his face and over his shoulder, expecting to see the woman from the pool with him. There's no one there. The speed at which Wolf moves through women is impressive and disturbing.

"You can join me if you'd like," I say despite my better judgment. "I promise I won't assume you're crossing an arbitrary line."

He settles in without hesitation and steals my menu. "Sounds good."

A deep breath later, I force myself to apologize. "I'm sorry for getting the wrong idea the other day. I just got out of something, and it messed with my head a bit." I don't want to give him more than that. He probably doesn't want to hear it anyway, and it's not an easy conversation to have, especially with someone who reminds me of the problem.

He doesn't respond. I'm sure I just made things way too awkward.

"Weren't you with someone earlier?" I ask. Because *that's* not awkward.

He peers up at me with a tilt of his lips. "If you're referring to my sister, she has a thing against driving at night, so she already took off."

Oh. There's an unwelcome flutter in my chest. "You amaze me," I say before taking a sip of my wine.

This gets his attention. He turns his body toward me. "Please continue."

I chuckle. "You're a big, bad rocker with girls who follow you into elevators and trample you after every concert, yet you're here alone, you declined an offer to party the other night, and, according to you, you haven't hit on me once. Either I'm losing my touch, or you are."

He throws back his head and laughs. It's nice and throaty, making me wish I could take back my frustrations with the male species and shove my tongue down his throat.

"First of all, I'm only refraining from flirting with you because you laid down the law the moment we met. But don't let your head inflate. My natural instinct is to flirt. It's what I do, whether you're my type or not. Second, I'm not alone. I'm with you. Which means you're not alone, either."

I let his words settle in before changing the subject. "Were you born in San Diego?"

"Born, bred, and raised."

"And you're staying in a hotel?"

His response is a shrug. *That's strange.*

It's his turn to change the subject. "Where are you from?"

"All over. Most recently, Seattle."

He sets the menu down and orders a whiskey water from our bartender before continuing. "My second favorite place in the U.S. Seattle kicks ass."

"Agreed."

"So then why are you touring? There are plenty of music jobs where you're from."

Coming from a musician, his question isn't that odd. Life on the road is a necessity for him. I have a choice. "I don't want to stay in one place. That's what I was doing when… Anyway, I want to travel. The road is where it's at for me. Visiting a new city every couple days. Always a new adventure."

"So was I wrong about you? When I said you didn't enjoy life?"

He doesn't have to elaborate. That conversation has been replaying in my mind—haunting me—ever since. "Life moves fast while we're on the road. Isn't that how it is for you? Watching life pass you by while you sit behind the glass of a tour bus?"

When he doesn't respond, I keep going. "We're just passengers on the road. We're life's bitch, and I rarely take detours. Never stop to smell the roses." I shrug. "Life isn't stopping for me, so I just keep moving through it. Isn't that what people call drive? Music is the one good thing. It carries me, and then it catches me when I fall." I stare into my plate, refusing to meet his eyes. That got a little deep.

"That's so … sad."

"Says the lonely rock star."

"I'm not lonely. Just because I turn in early one night doesn't mean I'm lonely. I'm surrounded by people. Constantly. How can you possibly call that lonely?"

I give him a look that asks if he's joking. He's either got a great poker face or he's in denial. "Wolf—is that really what people call you?"

"That's my name."

"Okay, then, Wolf. Being a musician—writing, traveling—it's the loneliest job ever. It doesn't matter that you're surrounded by thousands of people a day. Who knows you? Beyond the music. Who *really* gets you? Who can you trust and talk to every day? Who spends their days giving back to you what you give to the world?

Besides all that, you've got to be in your head most of the time and you miss out on everything else. Don't tell me you're not lonely. And don't tell me your band does it for you. They can't possibly be your everything. I'm sure it gets lonely as hell without having someone to share your stories with, to bounce lyrics off, to go sightseeing with you, to just get away for a while."

I'm not so sure I'm talking about Wolf anymore.

"I remember asking a certain someone to go sightseeing with me and she rejected me. If I really am lonely, it's not my fault."

I laugh, relieved the tone of the conversation has lightened. "It's my fault you're lonely?"

His upper lip curls at one corner. "Well, yeah. I guess so."

"Huh. I see. Well, then, I'm sorry," I say dryly.

He's smirking into his glass now. He thinks he's won. And I'm finding myself relaxing around him a little more than I'm comfortable with, so maybe he has. Damn it.

We order food and eat in silence as we watch the sports news channel above the bar. Even through the silence, my thoughts are loud, and so is my pounding heart. Wolf is a charmer. Even when he's just minding his own business, I'm a flurry over his presence. I took this job to get away from trouble. Not to run into more of it. I swallow my last bite and reach for my purse.

"I should get to bed." I shuffle out of my seat and throw cash on the bar.

His eyes move to my half-empty plate and then to me. He hands me back my money. "I got this, Lyric. I love your name, by the way."

My hand wraps around his fist to clamp it shut and refuse the money, and I know immediately that wasn't the best idea. Just the touch of his skin against mine alerts the swarm of flutters in my chest. I yank my hand away and step back. "Keep it for the tip."

He doesn't look up, just nods. "Goodnight, Lyric."

"Goodnight, Wolf."

Chapter Four

Wolf

After dinner I take my drink to the pool and slip my bare feet into the water. *Am I lonely?* Lyric asked the question earlier, and I keep coming up with excuses as to why I'm not.

I'm busy constantly. These next two weeks, I'll have more downtime than I've had in years. Usually not even a holiday passes without some type of obligation. I've gotten good at going with the flow and not asking for time off, because what would I do? Where would I go? I'm seeing the world on tour. I have my fans. My bandmates. My crew. Those guys are my best friends. Lyric's assumption that I'm lonely is way off. I just happen to love this life and take nothing for granted. Vacation isn't something I want or need.

A whistle of wind blows through the air, rustling something near me. I look to find a small piece of notebook paper fluttering, wrapped around a nearby chair.

The wind picks it up, and the loose paper is carried through the air until it skips across the cold cement. Right toward me. My first instinct is to reach for it, so I do. And then the words on the page catch my eye. I scan over them. It's a poem. Or maybe a song.

Guilt sweeps through me as I try not to take in the words even though the few lines I happened to catch are whispering through my mind on repeat. This isn't mine to read. But then who does it belong to? I look around to see if someone nearby could have dropped it, but there's no one else outside at this hour.

My eyes tilt down to the sheet in my hands and I allow myself to take in the words. From the first line, I'm sucked in. By the end of the first verse, my heart is beating faster. By the second, I know this isn't something anyone should leave for someone like me to find. These are lyrics. These words belong to a melody; possibly one that's unwritten.

Ten minutes later, I've reread it a dozen times and have started constructing a flow to the words, hoping a beat will follow.

Pulling my feet from the water, I take the piece of paper with me. It may not belong to me, but it sure as hell does not belong in the trash.

Once safely in my room, I set the mysterious sheet of paper on my dresser and flip on the television, hoping to drown out the words. I can hear the unwritten melody in my head. The chorus, addictive as hell. It's the same feeling I get when I've just written a great fucking hit. The problem is that I didn't write this. It's not mine to claim.

Growling, I throw the remote across the bed and walk to my dresser. With a glare, I snatch the words up and pace the room.

I should toss it.

It's not like I can actually do anything with these lyrics, except maybe get inspired. Looking down again at the words, I clench my jaw and inhale deeply. Maybe I can rewrite it. Use it as inspiration. That's all.

Harmless.

Relaxing my jaw, I sit back on the bed and lay the paper out flat, smoothing the creases my fingers left. It's been a while since I've written a great song. Something the guys—and I—would be proud to show off on the upcoming tour. I know it's what everyone wants, and because of that I'm not thinking clearly. But the pressure—it's insane. And writing isn't something I can force. At least not good writing.

For hours, I try to talk myself out of giving in to the riptide that has clearly stolen my senses. *What in the hell am I even thinking?* I should be knocking down every door in this hotel searching for the owner. But no, the most I do is search for the lyrics online to see if it—or at least something similar—already exists. When I was little, the quickest way to commit a song to memory was to copy the lyrics down on paper. It wouldn't be shocking if the owner of this sheet did the same.

The search comes up empty. Of course. And the lyrics are still reverberating through me as if they've already come to life.

So I give in. I succumb to the craving. And like with my own songs, I put pen to paper … and start editing.

♪ ♪ ♪

It's a few days later when I finally leave my room. That's what happens when I write a song—except I didn't write this one. I edited it and put music to it, but it's not mine. It belonged to a chair leg before the wind stole it and handed it to me. And editing is a strong word for what actually went down. There wasn't much I wanted to change.

Guilt rumbles through me at the thought of claiming it as my own, which is unfortunate. These lyrics are embedded in my soul as if I did write them.

I'm not a cover artist. Even purchasing songs from our producers is something I stay away from. That's not who I am. I've climbed the charts because I enjoy writing and performing original songs. No other song could possibly fit Wolf's sound. Except this one; this song haunts me.

It's noon, and I'm meeting the band at the studio we're renting for the day. We're having our first practice since our last tour ended, and it's much needed. The longer a band is together, the bigger the tendency to neglect the work that brought on the fame. I don't want that to happen to us.

We kick off the tour with a local show in one week, which gives us enough time to go over our set list and the lone new song I wrote during our last tour.

"It's too easy," Hedge complains after we play the new song. His reaction is not a surprise, unfortunately. My heart wasn't completely in this one, but Crawley had liked it. Hedge, however, is a perfectionist. He'll be the first one to tell me something is a piece of shit, and I love him for it. I just don't have a backup plan this time.

"What's too easy?" Crawley growls, setting his phone on mute and holding it away from him. We all laugh at the muffled voice of someone screaming at him on the other end of the line. All I can make out is "more money" and "we quit," which isn't even his problem to deal with.

"The set list," Hedge says. "We've done it a thousand times. Let's give this crowd something new. Something good."

"We've got 'Hidden Agenda,'" I respond halfheartedly, still trying to salvage my poor runt of a song. It's not a hit. Not even close. We all know it, but the guys have been keeping their mouths shut until now.

Hedge pierces me with his stare. "Oh yeah? You might be the face of this band, but we have a say, too, and we're not performing that piece of shit."

"Whoa." Derrick steps in. "Calm down, dude." Then he turns his gaze on me. "Do we have anything else to try? Maybe we should explore other options. We're not going to win 'em over with 'Hidden Agenda.' Sorry, Wolf."

His apology is unnecessary. He's right, and I'm only hurting the band by trying to make it work. Fuck.

Crawley's face grows red as he unmutes himself and places his phone back to his ear, ready to unleash on whoever's twisted his leg hairs. We all cringe in anticipation. We've seen him this irate before. "Tell those bloody wankers we have a contract! We are one week until show time, and they think they're going to stick us with an empty stage?"

I groan. A cancellation—that's what this is about. Crawley specifically requested this opening band, and now they're probably getting greedy. Wouldn't be the first time this has happened to us.

"Let the tour company deal with that shit, and get your head in this studio," I grumble at him.

Crawley is the best band manager we could have asked for, but sometimes I'm afraid his heart will explode when he's dealing with a crisis. He takes on too much and is the worst delegator, thinking he can do everything better if he does it himself—which is probably true, but it's not great for his mental or physical health. Or for his temper.

He glares in my direction, pushes buttons on his phone, and then waits for someone to pick up. I do my best to tune him out, but it becomes impossible when he says Lyric's name and something happens in my chest. *Shit.*

I haven't seen her since the night we had dinner at the bar. Then again, I haven't seen anyone. The mystery song quickly became my new obsession. The arrangement I composed for it is dark but hopeful, which is what our sound is about. The writing is simple but plays well to Wolf's natural sound. Heavy bass accompanied by an electric guitar and a whole lot of keyboard. My vocals would carry this one, since it's an up-tempo ballad. And the drums would hold everything together, filling in all the blanks. It could earn us another number one. I can feel it in my bones. For once, something took precedence over boobs and sex. And boob sex.

The itch I've been trying to suppress comes back in full force. I reach into my back pocket and pull out the flash drive with "Dangerous Heart" on it. I laid down the demo track yesterday to hear how it sounded. I wasn't going to play it for anyone else, knowing I didn't write the original lyrics myself, but I can't keep this to myself any longer.

I hand the stick to the sound engineer and then turn to face my band. "Look, guys. Do me a favor and take a listen to something. I think you'll dig it."

This gets their attention, and their frustration turns to anticipation. Hedge has everyone riled up about needing a new song. I can't disagree, but the guys are too hard on themselves. We always planned to play the same set list on both our West Coast and East Coast tours. The East Coast isn't expecting anything different, but the guys get bored easily.

Apparently so do I because I'm stealing lyrics from the hotel pool.

When the intro pours from the speakers, Crawley walks back in and takes a spot on the floor, lying down and folding his hands behind his head. His eyes are closed and the excess blood is draining from his face. He's listening. I watch the eyes of everyone in the room, anxiously waiting for their reactions—and kind of dreading them.

What if they hate it? Then I've wasted three days of my life obsessing over shit disguised as an opportunity for greatness. But what if they love it? It's not like we can fucking do anything with it.

The song is a bit slower than the ones they're used to, but that's a good thing. The label has been requesting something slow and catchy, and I've promised it to them. It's just not something I'm great at writing, come to find out.

But this … this just might be it.

Two wrongs don't mend hearts like ours
I give, you take, nothing feels right
Two wrongs can never break our fall
We're in too deep, losing sleep
Trying to forget what started it all

Angry eyes and brick wall armor
Lessons learned, paths paved, shield unyielding
A heavy weight, you'll never penetrate

And you won't be at the end of this story

Stay away with your dangerous heart
That damaged our love, that damaged me
Crushed to pieces, shredded flowers making art
You're dangerous, your soul is black
Dangerous heart, and I want none of it back

Can't rely on second chances
Since the first ripped me apart
You're not welcome here anymore
Cause there's no going back to the start

Stay away with your dangerous heart
You've damaged our love, you've damaged me
Crushed to pieces, shredded flowers making art
You're dangerous, your soul is black
Dangerous heart, I want none of it back

After the last line, the guys are staring at each other, excitement written all over their faces. They heard it. What I heard. A hit.

Hedge begins laughing. Crawley's eyes are wide as he leaps up from the floor as if it's bitten him. "This is yours?"

I hesitate for a second and wrinkle my nose. "Not quite."

The excitement in the room falls, and I quickly jump to my own defense. "I edited the lyrics, barely, and put it to music."

"Who wrote the original?" Lorraine asks.

My face twists as I reach into my bag and pull out the sheet of paper. "No clue. I found this at the hotel pool, fluttering around and lost."

"One man's trash is another man's treasure," Stryder says with a grin. "Sounds like you claimed something someone else didn't know what to do with."

I wince. "Not necessarily. Lost is different than tossed, man. We can't do anything with this yet. It's not mine."

"It sure as shit is yours. Where did you find it, exactly?" Hedge asks.

"It was wrapped around a chair leg, and the wind almost carried it into the pool. I caught it, but no one was there to claim it. But I don't know, man, someone could have another version of it somewhere."

Crawley tells the engineer to play it again, and the guys are silent. Some of their eyes are closed, and I know they're imagining us up on stage, singing "Dangerous Heart" to a mesmerized crowd. Meanwhile, my blood is pumping adrenaline like I've just taken the stage. It's only a rough acoustic version of what could be a badass track, but there's no denying we've got something here. If only we could get past the whole copyright issue.

"Can we find the person who wrote this? It's good, Wolf. Too good to just let it go, but you're right to be careful," Derrick says.

Then Crawley slaps Hedge on the back since he's the closest, causing Hedge to wince and squirm away. "I have an idea. Shit! I have a fucking brilliant idea." He's laughing and rubbing his hands together like a mad scientist. "We practice it and we play it at our shows—with a disclaimer that the unedited lyrics were found, and we're looking for the original writer. We don't release it for profit until we find them. This song will go viral. It's got to, and whoever wrote it will come forward to claim their share."

"Shit," we all say in unison. Sometimes Crawley comes up with ideas like this that remind us all why we hired him in the first place.

"Well, what are you shitheads waiting for? You've got a bloody song to learn." With another laugh and huge smile on his face, Crawley leaves the room, slamming the door on his way out.

Chapter Five

Lyric

Terese picks me up from the hotel early in the morning. She's accompanying me to Wolf's San Diego show and all the preceding activities for the day. I'm disappointed she won't get to come on the tour. She's the one cool chick I know who hasn't screwed me over yet. So far it looks like I'll be hanging with Lorraine and Stryder's girlfriend, Misty, a lot since we'll be sharing a tour bus. From what I can tell so far, we'll get along just fine.

And then there are the groupies. I've heard the rumors of how often they frequent Wolf's tour bus, and I'm trying to mentally prepare myself for that. The tags he gets on social media are telling enough, although it's obvious he's careful of his public image. He's far from innocent, but he's smart.

Terese and I arrive at the venue and immediately walk backstage to claim our badges. We're in an open-air arena tonight, so the only privacy for the band and crew lies within a cluster of tents and trailers.

The guys won't be here for a soundcheck until early afternoon, so we spend the morning stealing snacks from the VIP tent and perusing the band's surprisingly short list of demands. Where's the single-colored M&M'S and specific temperature water to accompany their classic porn selection? I expected Wolf's list to at least include his favorite condom brand. Then again, I shouldn't assume he bags it. Who knows how many of Wolf's pups are running around out there.

There are a couple of special requests from Lorraine and Hedge, but only because they apparently have food allergies. All-in-all, very boring.

"Lyric!" a voice calls from the other side of the dressing room trailer. I turn to see a familiar face grinning.

I hop up from the couch and pull Terese along, smiling brightly at the sight of him. Doug used to tour with my father as his road manager. Since my father was my primary guardian for most of my childhood years, Doug has always looked out for me like a second father.

It's only been a few years, but he's grayed since I last saw him. I guess the pressure of the job does that. But his face still carries his kind blue eyes and his boyish charm. Even at fifty years old, the man is a stud.

He pulls me in for a hug, squeezing extra tight like he would when I was a little girl. "Good to see you," he whispers.

My throat is jammed with emotion, but I'm able to blink back the tears when we break away from our embrace. "Hey, Doug."

"Congrats on the tour. This is a big one. Bigger than that Salvation Road crap band you were hanging out with back in Seattle."

I chuckle at his dig at Tony. I assume Doug knows about our relationship drama since he's practically royalty at Perform Live. He knows all.

"And don't worry," he says with a tilt of his lips. "They warned me you're just observing tonight. You won't have to put up with me ordering you around. But if you want to follow me to merchandise now, I can introduce you to the team."

"I'd love that." I reach for Terese's hand behind me and tug her forward. "Doug, have you met Terese? She works in local event promotions. She's my guest tonight."

He extends his hand. "Afraid we haven't met." They shake, and then we're taking the venue detour through the remaining tents and through the hidden backstage gate. Doug leads us to the merchandise booth the crew is setting up near the entrance.

"Why don't you two grab a Wolf shirt. On me," Doug says, getting distracted by a call coming in on his radio.

I smile, eyeing the collection currently in disarray on the table. We decide on matching black tees with Wolf's yellow logo splashed across the front and slip them on over our tank tops. "Nice," Doug says as he turns to introduce me to the crew.

"Lyric, this is Melanie, our merchandise manager. She's been with the crew for two years and is great at handling the crowd—and more importantly, their money. Her squad, Brad, Stevie, Raquel, and Patricia, will be traveling in bus number two."

Bus number two is the crew bus. It's got twelve bunks, one bathroom, and a small living area. It's the bus I thought I'd be on until Andrew informed me I was riding with the band. I've ridden with bands before so it's nothing new, but knowing I'll be sharing a small space with Wolf and his entourage makes my stomach churn. I'll have a front row seat to all the action. Not exactly something I'm looking forward to after leaving Tony.

Terese and I are following Doug backstage when a voice over his radio alerts him that Wolf has just arrived. We approach security, where Doug hands me a radio and places stickers of a purple cartoon wolf on our badges.

"What are these?" Terese asks.

I laugh at her confused expression. I don't even think about the secrets of backstage life anymore. I'm used to all the tricks of the trade.

"Once the venue doors open, the All Access badges only get us in the main backstage area, on the side stage, and into VIP," I explain. "The stickers get us anywhere else we want to go. Like the dressing rooms." I wink as her eyes glow with pride. "Don't you go backstage all the time?"

She laughs. "Not with free rein like this at a show as big as Wolf's. I handle smaller events and radio shows, mostly."

It's kind of exciting to show someone the ropes. "Come on. Let's say hi to the band." We walk out to the stage where the roadies are testing the instruments and microphones. Wolf is nowhere to be found yet, so we hang back and wait.

A familiar face approaches us, a pretty blonde in her early twenties, all done up. The radio badge gives her away, and my memory chugs to life.

"Jenn!" I exclaim with mock enthusiasm.

It's my job to network with the radio personalities since we're always promoting the band, and every now and then the band agrees to a little something extra to give back to their local fans. Local public figures like Jenn make those things happen. Most shows it's just a meet and greet backstage or a chance to win passes to watch sound check.

Unfortunately, Jenn has a reputation in the industry for taking certain relationships too far.

I dated a rock star, so I can't judge too much, but having a long-term relationship with someone who happens to screw you over two years later is a little different than a quick bang with every celebrity who lets you get close. Who wants to get kicked away and be forgotten?

Jenn's smile is warm and bright, making me wonder for a second if her reputation is undeserved. "I can't believe it's you, Lyric. Are you on tour with Wolf?"

I nod. "I am, but I'm not working this show. Just hanging out. This is my friend Terese," I say, pulling Terese forward. The girls greet each other. "Doug runs the show tonight. He hands over the reins after that, and then we're off to Raleigh. How are you?"

Jenn waves her arms around, her eyes wide. "Couldn't be better. This is the show we've been waiting for since we heard about it. Wolf has become the hottest thing in San Diego. I can't wait to see him again."

The way she says this with a wiggle of her eyebrows confirms my theory about her reputation—and his.

Jenn gives me a mock empathetic look, and I know what she's about to say. Here it comes. "I have to say, I'm surprised to see you here. After that last disaster." She makes a face. "I'm so sorry to hear about that."

Everyone in the industry knows about my latest breakup. The fans, not so much. However, the media has been starting to hint that the relationship seems to be rocky. I'm sure that with me being on Wolf's tour, it will all blow up. I couldn't care less.

Tony made sure to keep a seal on all relationship drama for fear that it would affect his tour. I complied because I didn't want the paparazzi up in my business either. They can be ruthless, and it's the last thing I need right now. With my parents so closely tied to the industry, whatever I can do to maintain a low profile is what I'll do. No questions asked.

Still, it's totally shitty that my heartbreak was on display for my peers. It's the one awful part of being so close to the industry and one of the many awful things about dating a rock star. There is no privacy.

"That's not going to keep me from the music, Jenn. C'mon, you should know better than that." I hold my smile, although it's the last thing I want to be doing now. She's just poisoned the conversation.

"Hey." Her eyes widen as if in afterthought, but I know better. "If you can help me snag an interview with Wolf, I would owe you big time. He wasn't able to come in to the station today, and his fans would *love* to hear from him."

"Sure, I'll see what I can do," I say, hoping by the time she tries to meet with Wolf we're already long-gone. The plan is to hit the road the moment the show is over. No meet and greets or anything fancy today. If Jenn wanted time with Wolf, she should have tried before tonight.

"Lyric, we need to go. Soundcheck is almost ready to start." Terese tugs on my hand. "Great to meet you, Jenn. Enjoy the show."

Terese and I walk away, and I squeeze her hand in thanks. She squeezes back knowingly. "How much you want to bet Jenn winds up in Wolf's bus after the show?" she whispers.

I laugh. "She can try, but there won't be much time for romping. We leave right after he gets off stage. Which reminds me, will you help me transfer my stuff from the car? I want to get it over with."

The group of buses is parked close to the backstage entrance along with the trucks full of gear. The only way I can tell the difference between the buses is by the slips of paper in each of the windshields. I'm with the band in bus number one. The rest of the buses, belonging to the openers I managed to convince to stay on tour, will meet us in Raleigh.

And what a shitstorm that was. Crawley has a reputation too. I guess everyone in the industry has some sort of reputation, but his gives me the creeps. The asswipe promised the opening act forty-five minutes of stage time, a tour bonus, and a per show fee, to be paid at the end of each show. But the dick "mistakenly" drew up the contract for thirty minutes of show time, no bonus, and one hundred dollars less, per show.

Even if the legal team did botch the contract like Crawley said, that gave him no right to argue with the band about it. They wanted to pull out, and rightfully so. But I got the label to create an addendum to the contract to give them what was originally promised and agreed to.

Problem solved.

Kind of. Crawley hates my guts. I get the feeling he didn't like me so much before, but now, I avoid sharing any space with him I don't have to. I can't explain it completely; I just know there's something about him I don't trust.

The transfer is quick and painless, but I'm disappointed I don't get to see the inside of the bus yet or pick out my bunk. I'll be the last one who gets a say on where I sleep, but I cannot be on the top. When I tried to tell Doug that, he told me I'd have to deal with whatever was left over, but he would put in a word with the driver, Rory, to try and save me a spot.

By the time we're done, soundcheck is almost over and Wolf is having a sidebar conversation with a red-faced Crawley. That guy is always angry about something.

My focus shifts when Hedge sees us and waves with exaggerated enthusiasm. "You girls look dead sexy in our shirts," his voice booms from the speakers.

Terese giggles, but my eyes catch Wolf's light brown ones as he turns his head toward us. We get a nod, and I return it, telling myself not to act stony. I have to remind myself of these things. He puts me on the defensive. We may have come to some sort of mutual understanding last week at dinner, but I want to make myself clear that I won't be one of his conquests. Still, I need to be careful. I'm not trying to make enemies. Plus, he's kind of my boss.

I can't hear what Wolf says before the band kicks off another melody. This one is unfamiliar but catchy. "Wait until you hear this new song, babe," Stryder says into the microphone. I look at Misty, who's grinning from her seat. She's clearly smitten, and I can understand why. Stryder has the lightest blue eyes I've ever seen, and the guy knows how to brighten a room with his energy. He is pure rocker, through and through.

I get excited at the mention of a new song. There's nothing I love more than the newness, before songs get overplayed. To my disappointment, though, all we get is the instrumental version. The soundcheck ends a few minutes later without so much as a "Check, check, one, two" from Wolf.

Wolf glances at us before hopping off the stage. I think he's headed in our direction. Derrick follows, his eyes all over Terese. He totally has the hots for her, and he's not even trying to hide it. Lucky for him, Terese isn't complaining.

Derrick makes it over to us, but Wolf is intercepted by Jenn. The disappointment I feel surprises me, and then it pisses me off that I care at all.

"I'll meet you backstage," I say to Terese, who's too consumed in Derrick to even acknowledge me.

As I slip backstage, Wolf's head turns and catches my eye, but he doesn't move. Of course not. That would be rude. Jenn works for the fans.

The problem is me. I am far too aware of all things Wolf in areas that surpass my job description. That acknowledgement sends me straight to the VIP tent, where I order a beer. I'm going to need a drink tonight. Perhaps many. At least then I won't care if I end up on the top or bottom bunk.

When the sex god himself appears next to me at the bar, I'm convinced he's following me. This is a test. If I can keep my libido in check around Wolf, I'll be blessed for eternity. If I give in to him, I'm headed straight to hell in the form of another heartbreak.

"Damn, woman. I wouldn't have taken you for a lush."

I glare at him over the rim of my beer glass. I *am* drinking faster than normal. "I'm not a lush. Just … anxious."

"About the tour?" As he leans over the counter, his broad shoulders roll forward to hold his thick, inked arms. A dark gray shirt stretches tight around his biceps and a ripple of his muscle makes me jump a little. He turns away for just a second to check out the beer selection, and that's when I let my eyes casually skim over his black denim-covered ass. *Damn.* Wolf doesn't need the illusion of the stage to make him larger than life. He's a solid guy. And tall. His hair is short at the sides but thick on top, currently styled like he ran his fingers through it several times, something I wouldn't mind doing for him if he wasn't *Wolf.* It's too bad he's a rock star because while I may not be his type, he's definitely mine.

"Lyric?"

My focus has traveled from his ass to his chest, and now it flickers to his mouth. Thank God he didn't catch me ogling him. I would never live it down. Then again, staring at his mouth is no better. Wolf has a nice mouth—full and juicy lips, outlined with just enough facial scruff to put to good use in my most sensitive places. Goddamn this boy is mesmerizing.

Finally, dragging my gaze back up, I know I'm going to lose. Whatever war is brewing between my head and the quick-building need between my thighs needs to end. I'm nearing the danger zone.

Wolf is gazing back at me, an amused expression playing on his face. "I think I'm going to like this tour a lot."

Heat rushes up my neck and I take in air through my nose, trying to ignore it. Turning to the bar, I order a second beer for me and one for Wolf, then start to walk away. After two steps, regret fills my head when I realize I never did answer his question. That was rude.

Pivoting to face him again, I slam into something hard. *Him.* What the hell is wrong with me?

He holds up his drink and laughs. "Forget something?"

I've never been so flustered in my life. In fact, I pride myself on being calm and confident, especially in situations like this. But Wolf simply defies all logic, and he's making me do the same.

"Shit, sorry. I just realized I didn't answer your question."

He's chuckling when he moves a hand to my face and swipes away a strand of hair caught in my eyelashes. "That's okay, darlin'. We all have our weaknesses. I'm yours. I get it." And then he walks off, grinning.

My entire head feels like it's about to explode, and I'm convinced he chose the wrong animal name for his band. Wolf is a jackass.

♪ ♪ ♪

I'm present, as in, at the concert, but I'm completely detached from everything I normally love about a show. The crowd is screaming like crazy as Wolf steps onto the stage and howls. That's his thing. He howls like a wolf, soliciting pandemonium from the crowd before diving into his opening number, "Joke's On You."

What a coincidence. That's exactly how I feel about myself right now. The joke is totally on me.

We're standing on the side of the stage, but I'm only here for Terese at this point. If it weren't for her, I'd be somewhere else, hiding out in humiliation, just wanting to sleep it off before the start of the tour. But no, I'm stuck here, listening to this raspy rocker light the open-air theater on fire.

Wolf's sound can be described as alternative rock that lends itself to both hard and soft. He tends to lean more toward the harder side of rock, but when he slows it down … damn. That's when I'm listening. His impassioned vocals tear me apart and then put me back together again, and it's impossible to ignore the vibrations his voice sends pulsating through me.

He's good at it all. Singing. Strumming. Strutting. The audience is eating out of the palm of his hand, singing along to every damn word of every song. Every song except for one.

I'll never admit this out loud, but I have every Wolf song memorized, and not because of this tour. I'm a fan of his music. Not him. *His music.*

But this song I don't recognize from their set list. It seems familiar, though. It's got to be the new one they teased us with during soundcheck.

Wolf begins to sing the first line of the song, but then he stops to get the crowd's attention. He's building anticipation.

Suddenly, the band stops too, and the spotlights focus on Wolf. "Did you hear that? That's our new single, if all works out."

A mixture of high-pitched woos and mangled screams take over the crowd. You'd think Wolf just proposed to a girl in the front row the way she's holding her mouth, eyes wide with tears streaming down her cheeks.

"But we have a problem," he continues, his voice booming through the speakers. "And we're gonna ask for your help."

This should be interesting.

"Full disclosure. These lyrics aren't mine. I found them recently, and I couldn't get them out of my head. We're about to perform it for you, and let me tell you, this shit is good." More cheering.

"We're going to play this song, but we need your help. Pull out your phones, your cameras, your iPads, what-the-fuck-ever you've got. Record it. Post it. Share it. If you wrote this gem, we're hoping you'll come forward. We're going to find our writer. But listen up," he booms, creating a louder roar from the crowd.

"This is no Cinderella shit. No impostors need apply. We aren't offering glass slippers or happily ever afters. We just want whoever wrote this song to come forward so we can make this single number one together."

Wolf gives the crowd time to soak this all up. I don't even know if they heard him over the screaming, but he's grinning and giving the band their cue to start. "All right, lucky motherfuckers. This is 'Dangerous Heart.'"

And then the beat starts back up, and I have to hold onto something. *That title*. I grab the rail in front of me, bracing myself to hear what has got to be a strange coincidence. But then I hear the familiar words as he sings the first line. My words. *Two wrongs don't mend hearts like ours.*

No fucking way.

Somehow, Wolf got his hands on my song. The one I trashed—for good reason. I should have never had to think about it again, and now he's playing it in front of thousands of people.

What the hell?

I want to scream as I rack my brain for an explanation. Did he see me toss it in the garbage?

Rage is starting to bubble inside me until I'm seething with anger, unable to see anything clearly. There's a ferocious beast inside me preparing to attack, banging down the walls of my cage, snarling and dripping with contempt.

There's nothing I can do but contain the beast. For now. But my fury only builds as I stand by, listening to Wolf sing my words to a crowd of thousands. Thousands of his dearest fans whom he's asked to make this shit go viral. And they'll do it. Because he's Wolf.

Chapter Six

Wolf

She's fucking crazy.

Jenn practically chases me from the stage the entire way to the bus and then demands a private interview, which Lyric has apparently already arranged without informing me. When we're alone, she stalks her way to the back of the bus where my bedroom is. I follow her, but only to tell her this isn't happening. Not tonight. Not with her. She needs to get the hell out.

"What the fuck are you doing, Jenn?" I practically explode. I'm already on fire from the concert, and while I usually like an easy lay, I'm not doing this with radio's best-known skank.

I'm a hypocrite, but I don't care. When I sleep around, it's not with girls who openly spread it for any musician on the planet. I have an ego that requires me to believe that the girls who wait outside my door are there for me and only me.

She's giggling, her arms around my neck, tequila and lime breath blowing in my face. "I said we had an interview. I was thinking we could get real *deep*." She grabs a handful of my cock and it immediately reacts.

"I appreciate the offer, Jenn. I really do." I grit my teeth to keep from giving in. "The bus takes off soon. No time." I gently pry her hands from the waistband of my pants, but she's fast, quickly wrapping her arms around my neck again and plastering her body to mine. She's like a leech. Her grip is so tight, and one of her legs has slithered around my waist. If she hadn't locked us in my bedroom, I could have called for backup. *Where the hell is Rex?*

There's a crash from outside the bedroom just as Jenn steps away to remove her top. Two perky breasts are now exposed, begging for me. *Fuck.* Her tits are nice, and it has been awhile. She sinks down to her knees, a wicked smile lighting up her face as she eyes my crotch and licks her lips.

If she sucks me off, I won't be returning the favor. I should let her know.

She has my fly undone in seconds and her hands are on my waistband, ready to unveil the goods. I want to tell her to stop gawking and get to work, but before I can open my mouth a small figure bursts through the door, eyes red as the devil.

Lyric. Gorgeous Lyric. She shouldn't have eyes of the devil but she sure as shit does right now. Her arms fold across her busty chest, and she glares at Jenn. "Put your tits away and get the hell out."

Jenn looks between Lyric and me, confusion written all over her face. And then disappointment, realizing she's not going to get what she wants. "Shit. Are you with Lyric? Why didn't you tell me?" She scrambles to her feet and tries to find her shirt.

Lyric takes a step forward, and I'm afraid she's going to throw a punch. I'm too turned on to stop her. "He's not *with* me, but that shouldn't make you feel better. Your tits are still hanging out. Leave."

"You can't tell me to leave." She glares at Lyric and then turns to me. "Right, Wolf?" Jenn gives it one last desperate attempt. I almost feel sorry for her and a little bit shitty about myself. Guilt isn't an emotion I experience often, but part of me hates that women like Jenn assume I'm a given, even though I kind of am. That's not the point. I take pride in my right to choose who and when and where I fuck. But chicks like Jenn think all they have to do is waltz in, strip, and my dick is theirs for the night.

As delicately as I can, I reach her shirt on the floor and hand it to her. "I'm sorry, Jenn, Lyric's the boss. We'll catch up when I'm in town again." *Not if I can help it.*

Lyric holds the door open—avoiding Jenn's death glare when she exits—and then slams it behind her. When she turns back to me, her eyes are still red and heated. It's my turn to get mad at her, but I can't. With anyone else, I would go off on them. If it was any other road manager, she'd be fired. But it's Lyric. And I find myself amused and a little bit aroused that she just kicked someone out of my bedroom.

She's still fuming, flushed and panting, and it's hot as hell. I've imagined making her cheeks that color more times than I can count. And I'm still hard. I shift slightly and she takes notice of the massive erection trying to fight its way through my boxer briefs. I quickly yank up the zipper of my jeans.

Too late.

Lyric gasps and looks up at me before squeezing her lids together and shaking her head. *Good luck purging that from your memory, sweetheart.* I snicker internally.

I thought she might have been hiding a little crush on me, but I had no idea she already wanted to stake a claim. I'll have to figure out how to deal with this for an entire tour—how to fuck her and then go back to business as usual.

"Care to explain why you kicked down my door?"

Her eyes move around my room until she spots something, and then she's moving to the set of drawers by my bed. What the hell? My eyes go wide. I run over and slam the drawers shut before she can see my pile of Polaroids, gifts from dirty girls who want to leave me with something to remember them by.

"Look, *Lyric*. I'm giving you a pass on barging in here because I didn't know how to let Jenn down gently. You saved me there. But I draw the line at going through my stuff."

She swivels, and I swear she's grown a few inches when she stares back at me. "Really? You have something to hide? You think you can steal intimate lyrics from people and then pawn them off as your own? Make a huge scene about it so that the world is on your side? You rock stars are all alike, aren't you? Caring only about yourselves."

"What the fuck are you talking about? Is this about that new song? I cleared it with Crawley and the label. We're ready to make a deal with whoever wrote those lyrics. They'll be set for life."

She squeezes her eyes shut, and it has a direct effect on my insides, like she's got my stomach in a vise. Just that look tells me what she hasn't said.

I've found my Cinderella.

"How did you find it? I threw it away." Her voice is still heated, but it's shaky now, hitting me straight in the chest.

"It's yours? Shit, Lyric. If I knew that—"

"What would you have done?" She glares, causing a sudden tightness in my throat.

This woman does things to me. And I fucking hate it.

"I would have talked to you before doing anything with it. I didn't know who wrote it. It was about to fall into the pool, and I caught it. If it meant so much to you, why did you throw it away? There was no name on it, nothing—"

"So you stole it?"

I shake my head, completely thrown off balance. "No. I didn't *steal* anything. Didn't you hear me out there? We want to offer you a deal."

She laughs, a sarcastic laugh, as if I'm insane. This is not the reaction I expected from the owner of those lyrics. Then again, I didn't expect the owner's name to be Lyric. There's a coincidence for you.

"Some things can't be bought, Wolf."

"I know that." I do. I absolutely know that. *Shit.* "Honestly, we thought we were doing a good thing."

"You didn't know it was my song?"

"No, I swear."

"You liked it?" Her voice is softer now.

That stops me in my tracks. I want to take her face into my palms and lay one on her. Is this insecurity coming from Ms. Feisty herself? "I love it, Lyric. The band loves it. Our manager loves it. The crowd fucking ate that shit up. We want it to be our next hit, and with the publicity we've brought to it tonight, we're well on our way."

Her eyes glaze over and shift away from me.

"Look at me," I say. She does. "I'm not just saying this... It's yours. If you want me to put a stop to it all, I will. If you want me to let the world know you wrote it, I can do that, too. Anything you want. Totally your call."

She looks at me, and by the way her eyes are scanning mine, I swear she's seeing me for the first time. It's possible. People get closed off when they've been burned; I know from experience. And Lyric's pain runs deep. So deep she couldn't see past the smoke when she first met me, but something is changing. Maybe she isn't ready to believe me, but she wants to.

There's a bang on the bedroom door, and Crawley's voice is low but clear. "We're taking off. Lyric, Wolf, you two in there? I need to see your faces before this bus leaves."

I roll my eyes and move to the door before Lyric can get to it. When the door is open, I see Crawley and Rex standing there. I make a mental note to talk to Rex later. He gives me a knowing nod and walks off. Crawley lingers longer than I'm comfortable with, glancing between Lyric and me, and then nods. "Thanks. See you in the morning."

"Wait," Lyric calls, stepping forward. I slam the door before she can leave. "What are you doing? I need to claim my bunk—"

"Not until we're done talking."

She shoves my chest, and I want to lift her up, making it easy for her to wrap her legs around my waist. Resistance makes for hot sex when it's consensual. "You can't imprison me."

"You can't kick girls out of my room."

"You can't steal song lyrics from innocent people."

"Then you shouldn't throw them away like they're nothing to you."

My breaths are heavy. We're only a couple of inches apart. My hands are itching to grip her waist and slam my mouth onto hers. Shut her the hell up, at least for a few hours. It might relieve some of the tension between us because, while it may have been questionable when we met, it's now painfully obvious. I want Lyric beneath me, wrapped around me, slipping and sliding with me until her moans turn to screams. I fucking want her. And I want her words, too. Her angry lyrics, her vulnerable confessions. I want it all.

"I don't want anyone to know I wrote it," she whispers, but she doesn't back away.

"What? Why?"

She shakes her head, ignoring my questions. "You can have it. You're right. I threw it away. It was too—"

"Real? Lyric, those make for the best songs. You should know this. It is real, and that's why I love it. That's why I became obsessed with it and holed myself up in my hotel room for a week. I can't write that shit. Not for lack of trying, but writing lyrics like that—the ones that come from life—real fucking life—taps into a part of me that I can't get to."

The softness that caresses her features tells me she understands. "You can. You're just afraid." She takes a small breath. "Please, don't tell anyone it was me. It's yours. No money. Just take it. I'll sign it over to you. Okay?"

"Okay." But I don't back down, and I don't remove my eyes from her although she's already looked away. I notice the way her long lashes flutter to the top of her cheeks. The way her small body is still shaking from the adrenaline rush of barging in here. The way she still stands straight, shoulders back, like a fighter. Lyric is a fighter, but she's also vulnerable, and I've glimpsed a part of her that makes me vulnerable, too. Her words. Her truth. I'm so totally fucked.

"I should claim my bunk." She looks up, begging me to let her go, so I open the door, although it's the last thing I want to do.

"Goodnight, Lyric."

She pauses and looks as though she's going to turn around. If she does, I might pull her back into my room, and this time I won't let her leave.

It's better if she leaves.

She's still facing away when she says, "Goodnight, Wolf."

Chapter Seven

Lyric

I'm awakened at the sound of my whispered name and a gentle gust of air scraping my cheek. A groan escapes. It's all I can muster. My body is heavy, my lids heavier. I'm not sure I could move if I tried.

"Lyric."

There it is again. I squint before opening my eyes, knowing whoever is waking me will appear blurry and asshole-ish. "You're on the couch and the guys are waking up. Come on, I'll take you to your bunk."

Ugh. That's right. My bunk. I open my eyes a bit wider to see a shirtless Wolf standing in front of me—the thief who stole a tiny part of my soul last night without even realizing it. To add insult to injury, there were no bottom bunks left by the time we were done arguing, so the couch was my only option.

"I can't sleep on the top bunk," I moan.

"What? Why not?"

I groan again and try to sit up, but my head immediately starts spinning—whether from the furious rage I spun into last night or from the few too many beers, I don't know. "I just can't," I say as I fall back onto the hard couch. My damn bones are going to hate me when I wake up for real.

"Come on, you can have my bed."

I'm too groggy and sore to move or speak again, so when Wolf takes me in his arms, I don't resist. In seconds, I'm poured onto soft, plush, fabric, and a blanket covers me. I curl into the mattress and let it form to my body. Before I can think about where Wolf has placed me, I'm headed back to dreamland.

♪ ♪ ♪

Too much silence. I've woken up on tour buses many times, and it's never been this quiet. My body is accustomed to the noise, and I can sleep through it like a baby. So why so much silence? There's a bright light through the thin skin of my eyelids, and I can tell it's well past morning. I also feel better rested than I have in a long time. And why the hell am I comfortable? Tour bus bunks are the furthest thing from luxury.

Nothing is adding up until I open my eyes and gasp. I throw the comforter from my body and sit up with a lurch. I'm in a bedroom on a moving bus. A bedroom?

"Morning, sunshine."

I gasp and turn toward the deep voice on the other side of the room. Wolf is sitting in a chair in the corner, his eyes glued to the television. He's watching a movie, but it's on silent. He reaches for the remote and presses a button, turning on the sound.

"Why am I in your bed?"

"You passed out on the couch and didn't look very comfortable. I tried to move you to a bunk, but you moaned about not liking it on top. Surprising. I took you for a woman who likes control of all things."

He's wearing a smirk, and I'd love to slap it off his face, but my body is screaming at me. I need to stretch, or run, but there's no room to do either. And I need to get out of Wolf's lair before he mistakes me for one of his groupies.

"I can't sleep on the top bunk—fear of heights thing. Ever since I was little, I've had horrible nightmares anytime I sleep high up. It's awful. I wake up constantly thinking I'm going to roll off. Not sure the boys would appreciate the screaming in the middle of the night."

Wolf nods, keeping his eyes on the television, which is now blasting with gunshots and curse words.

"What are you watching?"

"*Boondock Saints*. Ever seen it?"

Shaking my head, I make another move to stand. "No."

"Stay," Wolf says, surprising me. "It just started. It's actually a crime to have never watched this movie, so I'd like to help you out. Since I owe you for your song."

For a second I consider his offer, but then I remember why I'm on this bus. "I have work to do, phone calls to make, showers to take."

He looks at me like I'm lying. "There's nothing you're doing that can't wait two hours. Stay, Lyric."

His eyes dig into mine, and I'm frozen. Since when did my brick walls begin deteriorating for Wolf? We've known each other for what, two weeks? I'd like to think of myself as one of those girls who learns from her mistakes.

Wolf would absolutely be a repeat of something I do not want to experience again.

My decision to stay or leave is taking too long. All the while, I'm staring back at the guy who took my song and sang it to a crowd of thousands after asking them to make it go viral. Which reminds me...

"Speaking of owing me. Have you checked social media today?"

Wolf grins and tosses me his phone. I catch it easily.

"1.5 million hits on YouTube and counting," he says. "Looks like we'll have to figure out a way to break the news to the fans that we've found our writer but she wants to remain anonymous."

I look up. "Have you told anyone?"

"Not a soul."

Relief rushes through me as I watch the video. All I could see was red last night as the song played and my lyrics filled the theater. I'm still perplexed by how it all transpired, but even I have to admit the song is good—what Wolf did with it, at least.

"What's the deal, anyway? Why don't you want any credit for the song?" He's watching me. I can feel his eyes probing for a reaction. I give him nothing. Instead, I toss his phone on the bed, walk to the door, and turn around to face him.

"Can you pause the movie? I'd really like to shower and change before I crawl back into your crusty bed."

His eyes crinkle when he laughs. "You're insulting me. I love it. After offering you millions and then rescuing you from the couch and letting you drool in my bed. You're still insulting me. That's fine, Lyric. At least you're not screaming at me anymore."

I smirk and turn toward the door. "Day's not over."

♪ ♪ ♪

The moment the movie credits begin to roll, I turn to Wolf, ready to unleash my fandemonium and tell him he was right. But that doesn't happen because he's asleep in his chair, head propped against the wall, mouth hanging open. I laugh and tiptoe over until I'm directly over his ear. "Boo."

His eyes fly open, and I gasp when he grips my waist.

"Shit," he says when he realizes it's me.

My stomach is heaving with laughter. "I'm sorry, you looked uncomfortable. I'm going to get some work done now. You can have your bed back."

His hands are still on my waist, and his grip tightens as if he's about to tell me something. "Okay," he says instead, dropping his hands.

"Thanks for the movie."

I grab my laptop, pass the bunks, and head to the main living area of the bus. When I reach the kitchen, I see Crawley pouring himself a cup of coffee and spiking it with something from a metal flask. I chuckle and slip past him to set up my computer in the only available space left.

The guys take up most of the couch spaces, their eyes focused on different activities. Hedge has got his face in a book of poetry. I do a double take when I read the title: *Leaves of Grass*. Well, damn. I would have never pegged Hedge for a fan of Whitman, or a poetry connoisseur at all. Derrick and Lorraine are playing Grand Theft Auto, and

Stryder's busy nibbling on Misty's neck while she nibbles on a PB&J.

I get into the groove, plugging away on emails, making phone calls to the venue to confirm load times and ensuring shipments have arrived. Other than the music, this is what I live for. Creative organization. Managing chaos. I love every bit of it. I call the union teams to relay the confirmations and then call around to find dining options for the bands in the next few cities where we're stopping. We're hitting North Carolina first, and we'll be stopping at two hotels on the way to give the bus driver, Rory, a break and to let the guys stretch their legs for the night.

It's late afternoon by the time Rory pulls up to our hotel in El Paso, Texas. This is one of those times in my professional career when I worry. I worry that the band will have a fit when they see that there is no glamour in tight-timeline traveling. We should have left days earlier if we wanted to do this right. But the San Diego show was booked by their last road manager. I'm assuming it's one of the reasons he was fired.

Still, the band could have opted to fly into North Carolina, but Wolf wanted his bandmates and crew close leading up to the show. Maybe he has a thing for bonding time. I don't know. Not my job to worry once the lead singer demands something. I just make it work, even if that means less than five-star accommodations need to be booked.

No one says anything about the budget hotel as we gather outside the bus and stretch. The guys are too busy on their phones to notice much, anyway. Wolf collects his room keycard from me but doesn't take off right away. To my irritation, he follows me to my room and then smirks when I turn to face him at my door.

"Can I help you?"

His smirk turns into a frown. "So cold. I thought we were on the fast track to friendship after our movie date."

I purse my lips, begging my face to behave. "Your definition of friendship and mine are contained in two different dictionaries. And you don't date, remember?"

"Have dinner with me."

"You're serious?"

He nods, eyes gazing intently into mine. He's serious. "We've got three months together, Lyric. We might as well attempt to have a pleasant working relationship."

"Or what? You'll fire me like the last guy?"

He raises an eyebrow. "You heard about that, huh? That jerk deserved to get fired. He double-booked us twice and left zero time for Rory to rest. Scheduled the San Diego show the same night we're starting a new tour. He was an idiot."

Okay, that's pretty bad, even I have to admit. "I might screw up, too."

Wolf narrows his eyes. "Do you want to get fired? Look, Lyric. Believe it or not, I do have a say on who travels with me. I knew who you were, and I approved you to ride along. It had nothing to do with your looks, or your parents, or your insane songwriting ability. Obviously, I didn't know about the latter.

"Not to say I didn't have my doubts—with you being a female and all. Lorraine's the only chick I've ever shared a tour bus with for a reason. I let a beautiful woman on the bus, I know I'm inviting trouble. It's only natural one of these bastards will want to fuck you, and then what? Drama. But your reputation in the industry is stellar, and I only work with the best.

"Shit, just the fact that you talked our openers back onto the tour is enough to secure your job. But it's a mutual agreement. You can leave anytime."

"Really?" I didn't think that was the case with my contract at all. In fact, I remember reading pretty hefty rules regarding breach of contract. I'm Wolf's until he decides to kick me off his team.

"Really," he says.

I ignore the fact that I think he's lying. It doesn't matter. "I'm not going anywhere." My answer comes out so fast that I'm not sure exactly what I mean by it. Wolf admitted he approved me to be on this tour. I guess that means something to me.

"Good. Get ready for dinner. I'll swing by to get you at seven."

Chapter Eight

Wolf

There are sexy women and pretty women ... and then there are drop-dead gorgeous, beautiful women. Lyric Cassidy is all the above. She's wearing the most unforgiving tight jeans and T-shirt ensemble. Her hair is thrown up in a messy bun, and her face looks as though it's just been washed. No makeup. She's not even trying, which makes her even sexier. I'm sure it's some ploy to distract me from her fucktastic body. Joke's on her.

"Where to?" she asks, shutting the door and facing me. Before I get a turn to speak, she gasps. "Shit. I didn't get us a car."

"You're fired."

I feel like a dick when her face blanches and her mouth falls open.

Chuckling, I lift my elbow for her to take hold of. "I took care of everything. You're off duty tonight."

She glares before hooking her arm around mine. "I'm never off duty. Besides, this isn't a date."

My chuckle rolls into a laugh. "There's that word again. We should get something straight right now. You don't have to worry. I sing. I fuck. I eat. I don't fall in love, Lyric. I don't date. I don't play games either. You can always count on me to be straight with you. Some women find it refreshing; others hate it. You strike me as the type who might find me refreshing." I wink at her.

"A bad boy who is honest and doesn't fall in love. Interesting combination."

"Thanks to my amazing mother and dirtbag father, I'm a hybrid."

We're silent the rest of the walk to the car, which is waiting for us at the curb. Rex slips into the passenger seat and I turn back to Lyric. By the look on her face I can tell she's thinking, probably about what I confessed about my parents. It's not exactly a confession, but it's telling enough. I know that. I've never hidden the fact that my father wasn't around when I was growing up, but I usually leave my mother out of things. It's not her fault that my father disappeared on us, that she spent a good portion of her life silently heartbroken.

She hid her pain to protect my feelings, but I knew. As hard as she tried to be the perfect role model, I wanted to hunt my father down and hurt him for what he had done to her. I still shake with emotion every time I think of the day I went through her call log. My heart felt as if someone had used it as a punching bag. So many attempts to reach out to him. All unanswered. No return calls. He just ... disappeared.

It's not even like my dad was the biggest rock star. He was the drummer for an okay eighties throwback band. It was cute when I was younger, but the older I got, I realized they weren't a band that would ever take themselves seriously. They wanted the lifestyle, not the hard work.

We slide into the backseat, Lyric first, and I signal to the driver, letting him know we're ready to go. It's then that I face her and smile, hoping to bust through the tension. "It's nice to go to dinner with someone other than the band for once."

She's smirking, and I know whatever she's about to say will make me regret my last sentence. "Maybe you should rethink your no-dating rule. You'd get out more and, you know, get to know people. Preferably before they sneak onto your tour bus and go down on you."

I almost choke on my own air as I breathe. "I have nothing against taking a woman out to dinner, but then it might give the impression that I want more than just food and sex. That's never the case."

"You're having dinner with *me*."

"You're safe."

Her face falls but hardens quickly. "Never? There's never been a female you thought maybe, just maybe, could turn you from One-Night-Stand Man to Monogamy Man? I find that hard to believe."

"Monogamy Man sounds like a disease. No wonder I'm not suited." She doesn't laugh at my awful attempt at humor, so I shrug. "You don't have to believe it, but it's true."

"You use women."

"Women use me."

She scoffs. Her mouth is hanging open in shock and maybe a little disgust. "Most of the women you sleep with are probably hoping for something more, but they're content with what they're getting at the time. I've never understood how one-night stands can end well, ever. One person has got to be into it more than the other."

Okay, now she's hooked me. I give her my bewildered stare. "You've never had a one-night stand?"

She shakes her head as if I'm the crazy one. "Absolutely not. Someone is bound to get hurt."

"Not from one night. That's the point. It's a one-time event, a release of pent up energy. It has nothing to do with feelings. Feelings stay out of it, and it's just a good time." The more we talk about sex, the more I want to prove to her how great a one-nighter could be.

We pull up to the curb in front of the restaurant before I can shove my foot in my mouth. I help Lyric out of the car. She looks up in surprise at my chivalry and then smiles. *I'm not an asshole.* I want to tell her this, but we're escorted into the restaurant and to our private table in the back of the room faster than I can speak.

"Is it this bad?" she asks, peering around us in bewilderment.

I cock my head as I pick up the drink menu. "Is what this bad?"

"You. Getting recognized. Having to request special accommodations everywhere you go."

I shrug. "If I want privacy, it's necessary."

She lets out a rush of air, and I think I've finally succeeded in impressing her. At least for a moment. "You really are a rock star, aren't you?" She smirks into her menu. It's infectious. I smile, too.

A moment later, we're ordering a bottle of wine and appetizers and talking about the tour. Somehow we get onto the subject of the crew. There are more than two dozen people on our tour, and she already knows every single one of their names and job descriptions. I don't think she studies this shit.

I get the distinct feeling that she simply has a superb ability to listen and retain information.

After ordering our food, there's a pause, so I jump in with a question I've been wondering since we left San Diego. "You still writing lyrics, Lyric?"

"Don't do that." She cringes. "It devalues me."

"How so?"

"Your name is Wolf. Does that mean you love wolves? It's an expectation that wouldn't exist if we were named something else. It just so happens I love music and write songs. My name has nothing to do with that. However, since my name is Lyric, it's implied that I should love music. That I should write lyrics."

"Names can tell a lot about a person. I'll have you know, wolves have a sharp intelligence and strong instincts."

She smirks. "Wolves also symbolize fear and distrust." She cocks her head. "Maybe you're right. Names do tell us a lot about a person."

Interesting. So, she's been looking up the meaning of my name. I'm certain she didn't come up with that on the spot. My eyes wander across her face, down the base of her throat, and to the rise and fall of her chest before returning to her lips. Those kissable lips. I shake my head, biting back another laugh as I clear my thoughts. "I see you've put a lot of thought into this. How about you just answer the question?"

"I am always writing lyrics." She says it quietly, confessing. "Since I was a little girl. I never kept a journal, just a songbook. I write poetry and lyrics."

"Do you play any instruments?"

She freezes. I catch the moment of fear that splotches her chest, and then she breathes through it as if it were nothing. "It couldn't be avoided when I was younger. Usually when parents shove something down a kid's throat, the kid rebels. Not me. I learned piano first and then guitar, and I loved every second of it. But I haven't played in a while."

"You really are a marvel, aren't you?"

Lyric makes a face. "Not quite. Disappointment is a better word for it."

I want to lean over the table, take her face in my hands, stare deeply into her sage-colored eyes, and tell her she's crazy. Instead of terrifying her, I remain in my seat, but I decide to let her know what I'm thinking. "You, Lyric, are the furthest thing from disappointment. Whoever helped you reach that conclusion is the problem—not you."

She takes a sip of her wine, not tearing her gaze from mine. "My parents had expectations. I couldn't fulfill them."

"Couldn't? Or didn't want to?"

"Does it matter? Perception is everything."

Her eyes gut me. They're terrifying and beautiful and honest. I'm not sure if Lyric could hide an emotion if she tried. Not with such transparent armor.

"There is a difference. You could have fulfilled their expectations, but maybe you realized you'd rather fulfill yours."

Her cheeks turn a rosy pink. "That's what I'm doing. At least I think that's what I'm doing. I don't really know. It's nice being around the music 24-7, but I'm not sure what's in my future."

"Don't worry about that. You're doing what you love now. The rest will fall into place."

I watch her as she takes this in, wondering how on earth her douche of an ex could have traded her in for someone else. Whoever he cheated on her with must have had some magical pussy juice because Lyric is insanely hot, smart, and fun to be around. I've never felt so comfortable around a chick before. Not like this. Sleeping with someone is one thing, but talking to her, having her open up to me, is a whole other level of friendship I've never had with the opposite sex, besides Lorraine—but she doesn't count since she's like a sister to me. I can see that Lyric will change my opinion of the female species. Maybe she already has.

Conversation flows through dinner as I learn about the places she's been and the places she wants to go. She tells me about the first song she ever wrote.

"It was called 'Star Light.' I was eight. My dad used to tell me that if you looked hard enough, you could find messages in the sky. It was silly, but as a little girl I clung to that. When he sent me to live with my mom, I'd stare at the sky every night, thinking maybe he was looking too. That way we would still be connected, somehow." Her eyes are hazy for a second before she shakes her head and smiles. "Sometimes I still look up."

I swallow, surprised by the tightness in my chest.

"Where do you get your inspiration when you write?" she asks.

I shrug. Something about Lyric makes me feel like I can trust her with anything, but I'm not sure I have an answer to give her. "It depends. You know well that inspiration can strike at any time. I've actually been having trouble writing lately. Maybe being off the road has something to do with it. So I'm hoping it comes back. The guys are begging for more."

She seems to be considering my words. "It will come back." She smiles, stealing my breath. "I can feel it, Wolf.

Your inspiration will be found on this tour. You've only just begun."

Funny. As she says this, I wonder if I've already found my inspiration. Maybe it's sitting across the table from me.

Chapter Nine

Lyric

The gym is empty when I pop my head in early the next morning. We don't have to leave until nine, so that gives me two hours to work out all the energy I have before we're stuck on a bus for the next ten hours. I unzip my light sweater and hang it near the door before climbing onto the elliptical for a warm up. After five minutes, I grab a mat that's propped against the wall and start stretching.

As much as I love touring, it doesn't change the fact that I'm an active person by nature. Always have been. I wasn't the best at sports, but I enjoyed them and joined the track team in high school. That's where Joanna and I became fast friends. We both loved the idea of organized team sports, but we didn't take home any trophies. Didn't care to. We stretched together, ran together, and tied for last place like it was our job.

Chuckling at the memory, I stand and walk to the treadmill on the other side of the room. The gym is big enough to hold three cardio machines, a complete weight set, a stretching area, and a wall for free weights in front of a floor-ceiling mirror. Decent enough for letting off a little steam.

I've just reached a jog on the treadmill when the gym door opens and Melanie walks in. It's the first time I've seen her since we were introduced at the San Diego show. "Hey, Lyric," she says with a smile. "Another gym whore like me, I see."

I laugh and shrug. "It's a necessity. I didn't start working out until I started touring after college. When I was a kid, I traveled with my dad everywhere, but the bus was like a jungle gym then. Not anymore."

Her eyebrows raise. "That's right, Mitch Cassidy's daughter. Would it be weird if I told you I've had a crush on your dad since I was eight? Posters on the ceiling and everything."

Groaning, I try to laugh through the unease after hearing that. "You totally could have left that fact out of this conversation. Pretty sure he's got at least twenty years on you."

Her eyes twinkle with mischief, and already, I have a sense of who Melanie is, beyond just our merchandise manager. From the little we've spoken and everything I've heard from Doug, I can tell she's a nice, honest, unashamed rebel who gets shit done. I like her already.

"Age doesn't matter, honey," she says. "Sooner you figure that out, the more plentiful your options will be."

My smile is huge. Melanie and I are going to get along just fine. "Are you here to work out or give me dating advice?"

She shrugs as she takes the machine next to me. After setting the machine to a warmup pace, she tosses me a grin. "I hear you don't need any dating advice."

"What does that mean?" I ask, my voice dropping with regret. One dinner with Wolf and everyone knows? They'll most likely assume we're hooking up, and my reputation on this tour is shredded before I even have a chance to prove myself. Because I know I need to prove myself. Being a chick road manager, I have to show the critics that I'm the shit at what I do. There's a reason I'm in my position, and it has nothing to do with my parents.

"It means," she draws out, "you seem to be a magnet for the hot lead singer types. First Tony, now Wolf."

I start to argue, but she cuts me off with stern eyes and a shake of her head. "I'm not blind, Lyric. I see the way Wolf devours you with his eyes. Did you know he told Hedge to stay away from you? I've never known that one to be territorial, but if I were you, I would totally jump on that meat stick."

Geez. She doesn't beat around the bush, does she? As I increase my speed I contemplate how I'm going to end this conversation. Melanie has no idea that this topic is dead. There is no Wolf and me. "Thanks for looking out, Mel. It's okay that I call you that, right?"

"Everyone calls me Mel. It's perfectly fine. Hey, Lorraine, Misty, and I are making an appointment to get our hair and makeup done when we get to North Carolina. You should come with."

And just like that, the conversation moves back to the safe zone. "Count me in. I'll need some pampering when this three-day haul is over with."

"You're telling me," she laughs. "At least you get to look at shirtless rock stars all day. I get sweaty roadies who refuse to shower until we stop at the hotel. Even then, their hygiene is questionable."

Laughter bubbles up my throat. "There should be a rule about that."

Her eyes go wide. "There is! But what's going to happen to them? You're the road manager now, what are *you* going to do about it? I dare you to tell Jeff his pits stinks and he needs to keep his shirt on when he leaves his bunk. No one needs to see that much pale skin in one eyeful. He's like the sasquatch version of Casper, minus the hot blue eyes and infectious laugh."

"You have a thing for Casper now? Mel, I think you're the one that needs dating advice."

When she glares at me I stick my tongue out. That's when the door to the gym opens again. Derrick, Hedge, and Stryder walk in, and my chest tightens, knowing Wolf will follow. He does, looking hotter than ever in a sleeveless white tank, dark gray basketball shorts, and bedhead. My heart beats a little harder when his eyes catch mine.

"Ladies! Mind if we join you for a little workout?" Hedge jumps behind Melanie on her treadmill, keeping in time with her steps and tugging on her hair.

"Jesus, Hedge! You fall, she goes down with you. You know that, right?" Derrick scolds him, only bringing a wide smile to Hedge's face.

Hedge sighs heavily and hops off the machine. He walks to the bench press, making sure to punch Derrick in the arm as he passes. "Fuck off, Dad."

I bite my bottom lip as Melanie rolls her eyes and increases her speed to a full-out run. Someone's showing off.

Not me. I'm taking my workout on the road. The blue Texas skies are calling to me anyway.

I stop my machine, wipe it down, and wave at Melanie before gripping the door handle.

Wolf cuts me off, sliding between me and my exit, and my chest begins to tighten. "If we're bothering you, we can go. You don't need to leave."

"Aww," Melanie calls from across the room. "Wolf and Lyric are twinsies. How cute."

I look at Wolf again and realize we're both wearing white tops and gray bottoms. Awesome. My face heats and my eyes find Hedge, who is full-on glaring at Wolf. Derrick is doing a fine job of ignoring us all, and I like him even more for it.

"Uh, no." I turn back to Wolf to answer with a smile. "I was just warming up for my run. Gym's all yours."

He nods and opens the door for me, letting me through. "I was thinking about a run, myself. I'll join you."

Is this guy for real? First he steals my lyrics, then he takes me to a friendly dinner, now he wants to run with me? Isn't he my boss? Well, technically, he's my client who pays me to boss him around. I should appease him, but at what point are we crossing the line? Running with him would be harmless if I didn't find his bedhead sexy as hell.

"Do I have a choice?" I ask with a grin, because let's face it. Wolf will do what he wants.

He shrugs. "Not really. To be honest, I'm not a fan of letting cute girls roam strange city streets alone. You're either running with me and Rex, or you're taking Rex with you."

Aww, he's playing the protector card. I like it. And if he hadn't mentioned Rex I wouldn't have even noticed him walking a good ten feet behind us. "He is stealth," I say, impressed.

Wolf chuckles, throwing Rex a nod. "That's what I pay him for."

"I thought you pay him to protect you."

Wolf shrugs. "If anyone were to try to mess with me, they'd be sorry. Rex is the result of a few stalkerish incidents at the start of my career. The label demanded I hire someone, so I did. He's become more of a prevention tactic than anything. The ladies love him, but he won't fuck around with them. And he distracts them so they stay away from me."

My eyes go wide just as we exit onto the street of the hotel. I immediately throw myself into a jog, and Wolf picks up the pace so he's right beside me. "You're kidding. Wolf needs a deterrent from the ladies? Isn't that your thing? I mean, I'm pretty sure I saw you in action when I walked in on you and Jenn."

He laughs, and I can feel his eyes on me. "I didn't want to sleep with Jenn."

"That's not what it looked like to me."

He lets out a breath that resembles frustration. "I'm not as bad a guy as you want me to be, Lyric. Who I sleep with and how often shouldn't define me. Just like your relationships shouldn't define you."

Discomfort settles deep in my stomach. I'm not sure why I care so much about any of this. I shouldn't. "You're right. We should talk about something else. Something that will help me get to know you better."

Silence falls on us and I can feel his eyes on me as we pace each other. "Okay. Ask me anything."

103

"Okay. What was the first song you remember that inspired you?"

"Easy. 'Sex On Fire' by Kings of Leon."

My head snaps toward him in surprise and I almost miss a step, but Wolf grips my waist to steady me.

"You're kidding me," I say, ignoring the buzz that shoots through me the moment his hand touches my bare skin.

He laughs. "I'm not kidding. I was a horny kid, and the song had the word sex in it. I could picture myself singing that same shit on stage."

"Okay, so 'Sex On Fire' inspired you to be a sex god on stage. What about, inspired your life?"

His face scrunches together as he thinks. "3 Doors Down. Same year. 'It's Not My Time.'"

My smile widens and I nod in approval. "Much better."

When Wolf starts belting the lyrics of the song, I'm laughing so hard I have to slow my pace.

"What about you? Same question, but your 'dad's music doesn't count."

I don't have to think long about that one. "'A Moment Like This,' Kelly Clarkson."

Now it's Wolf that almost trips, so I slow my steps and laugh as he catches himself. "I thought we were being serious."

I shrug. "I am dead serious. First song to inspire. I wanted to be Kelly Clarkson, once upon a time. Those raspy R&B vocals that can take you low or high. She's incredible."

"But 'A Moment Like This?'" he asks incredulously. "It's the most overproduced, overplayed radio song on Earth."

I laugh, knowing he's right, but I don't care. "We're being honest. That's my song. Believe me or not. I won't take it back."

"Faster?" I ask him, ready to tear down the street.

He winks. "Ladies first."

Our slow jog turns into a run, and not ten minutes later we're racing, huge smiles on our faces as we fight laughter and sprint to the end of the next street. I'm not sure who wins.

We're both heaving, palms on our knees and trying to catch our breath. I don't think either of us paid attention to where we were running to, but when we see a corner café beside us, we look at each other in silent agreement. "Coffee," we say in unison.

Wolf lets me walk through the door first, his hand automatically moving to the sweaty small of my back. I cringe, knowing I must look and feel disgusting, but his hand stays on me until we reach the counter to order.

"Okay, Kelly Clarkson," he teases when we sit on the padded bench in the corner window, coffee in hand. "I think you just outed yourself without meaning to."

My chest tightens at his words. "Excuse me?"

His lip curls at the corner just like I hate—and love. "If you loved Kelly Clarkson, that means you were an *American Idol* fan, and everyone knows *The Voice* is better."

My jaw drops for two very different reasons. One, his assessment went the total opposite of where I thought it would go, and two... "Excuse me. *American Idol* was the original singing contest that allowed America to weigh in on the winner. I choose originality."

His eyes roll dramatically. "C'mon. The talent on *The Voice* is better."

I shake my head. "Not necessarily. Their talent is hand-picked from singers already in the industry in some way. Magic lost."

"Oh really? And you think Simon really sat through every single audition so he could tell every kid in America that they were better off working kitchens than pursuing their dreams?"

Shrugging, I take a sip of my iced vanilla latte, the cold liquid cooling my overheated body, and bite my bottom lip. "He was a little harsh, but at least he wasn't sugarcoating everything. Honesty means more, even if you don't like it right away."

Wolf's eyes find mine. Our shoulders are butted up against each other, his hard and bulgy, mine soft and still very sweaty. I swallow against the roll of my stomach.

"I agree," he finally says. "Honesty does mean more. Which is why I should probably tell you that sweat and a white sports bra is an epic combo. One I hope you'll carry forward every single day of this tour."

My hand shoots out and smacks his chest. He laughs, but catches my hand. "Don't be an asshole. I was just starting to like you."

"Really?" His brows shoot up and I immediately regret my statement. When I try to pull away he tugs me closer and wraps his hand around mine. "Sorry about the comment. I couldn't resist."

My cheeks feel like they're on fire, but I'm not sure if it's from flattery or embarrassment. Wolf has me all kinds of confused.

It's not until I stand that he releases my hand. He tilts his head, locking eyes with mine. "What do you say, Lyric? Should we head back?"

I think he just likes saying my name. Or maybe it's me who likes hearing it. Fuck, I don't know anymore. Each time his tongue lingers on the L a little too long, flutters erupt in my chest. I nod and take a step back.

We decide to walk back to the hotel, all the while playing a game of Guess the Release Year. Wolf wins when I can't get "I Stand Alone" by Godsmack, but it's a close one. Wolf's bandmates are already boarding the bus when we arrive, and we have to rush to the twelfth floor to shower and pack our things. But before I can step into my room, Wolf places a palm on my room door, blocking my entrance like he loves to do. "I had fun today."

I smile, because so did I. "Ditto."

His lip curls. "You've kind of screwed yourself if you weren't looking for a new running partner."

I shrug. "Keep buying me coffee after, and I think that arrangement will work just fine."

His grin is full, melting my insides. "Deal."

He holds out a hand to shake, and I stick mine out.

I don't think I can lie to myself anymore. The moment our palms connect it's like an electric current awakens something in me. I felt it before, but I wouldn't let myself hold onto it. This time, I hold on for dear life.

Chapter Ten

Lyric

The tour kicks off on Thursday at the PNC Arena in Raleigh to a sold-out crowd. Eighteen thousand attendees are already filtering into their seats around the end-stage, purchasing beer, taking selfies of themselves and the empty stage, and crowding the halls near the merch booths.

I'm wearing my black Wolf tank and white, high-waisted skinny jeans with rips at the knees. My black, low-heel ankle boots give me more comfort than style since I'll be walking the venue like a madwoman. I use the office backstage to print the final VIP and backstage lists that security will use to double check everyone with a badge.

The band should be arriving any minute, so I head to their dressing room now to make sure they're stocked with the essentials. They like to be at the arena one hour before showtime to greet the opening act, shoot the shit, and get pumped for the show.

Simply Red, the openers, have an emotionally-driven rock sound much like Wolf's. They were a great pick to open the show, but I'm surprised there isn't more comradery between the two bands. Crawley doesn't hide his anger toward them for almost walking from their contract, which is crazy, since it was his fuckup—not theirs. But his aggression has spoken volumes, enough for them to keep their travel schedule as distant from ours as possible. It's unfortunate, really.

I understand the importance of being an opening band on a crazy popular tour like this one. Wolf's name could take Simply Red to places they never dreamed of, but with an awkward relationship, it makes their journey so much harder. As much as it bothers me, it's not my place. I saved the opening act from walking away, and that's really all I can do.

Stepping into Wolf's dressing room, I eye the stocked bar and check it for the band's favorites. Johnnie Walker, Chivas, Patron, Voss water. Check. Next I check their snacks. Miniature dark chocolates, pistachios, gummy worms. Check. They also asked for sandwiches for their dinner and and shower gel for their after-concert showers. I laugh when I see something new on the menu. Iced skinny vanilla latte.

Since when do the guys drink skinny lattes?

"Miss Cassidy, hi," greets one of the room assistants. She's cute, probably still in college, with bright red hair and the bluest of blue eyes. She's gorgeous, and the guys will agree. Panic swirls in my stomach when I think of Wolf laying eyes on her.

"Hi," I say with a forced smile. "You must be Rachel."

Her smile widens. "That's me. Would you like your latte now? I can run to the bar and grab you one."

My eyes widen and I check out the drink menu again. I mean, I always grab my coffee from the bar myself. Someone thought to put it on the menu. "Do you know who added this?"

Rachel smiles when sees what I'm pointing at. "Wolf called earlier today. We just printed up a new menu. It was no problem at all."

I nod, feeling slightly off-balance at Wolf's thoughtfulness. I guess he's always been considerate in his own way, but it's getting harder to ignore. "I would love one, thank you."

Rachel exits the room just seconds before the guys enter. Hedge sees me first and runs over, his hair bouncing around his head as he moves. I laugh as he wraps his arms around my waist and swings me around. I don't have to sniff hard to smell the tequila wafting from his pores.

"Hedge, have one of these," Wolf says, coming up behind us and handing him a water.

Hedge shoves him away in annoyance and hugs me tighter. My eyes bulge in confusion. "You fucker. You just don't want me to hug Lyric."

Wolf slaps a hand on his shoulder and yanks him away. "You're drunk. Drink this and get your shit together. First show, man. First show."

Derrick approaches for the assist, slinging an arm around Hedge and turning him away. "Let's check out the venue or something, man."

Hedge behaves as he takes a pull from his water, but not before throwing Wolf a glare over his shoulder.

"What was that about?" I ask, following Hedge with my eyes until he and Derrick have left the room.

Wolf shrugs. "He's just excited about the show. Drank a little too much back at the hotel."

Rachel comes back into the room, stepping past Misty and Stryder, who are fondling each other by the door. She hands me my latte, but her eyes are roaming over Wolf, assessing every detail. And liking what she sees. My stomach rolls.

Wolf's eyes never leave mine when she approaches, and it pisses me off that I'm satisfied by knowing he doesn't even see her. Yet.

In the last couple of days, Wolf and I have struck up a friendship of sorts. He's made good on his promise to run with me in the mornings during our hotel stays, and we've made it a habit of sneaking in movie time while I'm supposed to be working. He's even shown me a couple of new songs he's been writing, and I've given him my honest feedback. He likes the critiques. He says they push him to do better. And I honestly believe he wants my approval, though I'm not sure why. He's Wolf. He's known for his original songs that are the heart-pumping kind of addicting.

I do my best to shake all thoughts of Wolf from my mind because it's almost showtime and I'm on the clock. I fist bump each of the guys and walk out of the dressing room before them. Watching a band's entrance is one of the most exciting thrills of the backstage experience. The entourage that surrounds them. The roar of the audience that awaits. And the silence that fills the air in anticipation, heard only by those in the corridor between the dressing room and the mainstage floor.

I wedge myself against the corridor wall between two excited bodies, and I wait. Not ten seconds later, the dressing room door bursts open. Venue security leads the trail of band members, along with Crawley and a couple of roadies. They make their walk to the stage to start the intro, and as they do, I can feel the energy shift from anticipation to borderline insanity. The crowd knows what—who—is coming next.

Wolf is the last one out of the dressing room, followed by Rex and another security guy. Wolf looks charged up as he focuses on the walk, almost like a boxer making his walk to the ring to fight a title match. He's completely in the zone, so much so that he ignores the pleas from the corridor crowd to look their way. The man is on a mission. So when he nears me and his eyes slip to mine, air freezes in my throat. It's only a second, a moment, but he sees me. Then he winks before turning forward again, like it was nothing.

But it was everything.

♪ ♪ ♪

The fan meet and greet lasted longer than expected, so I assume that the moment we finally jump in the van to take us back to the hotel, we'll crash and prepare for an early call time in the morning.

But that's not what happens. Instead, Hedge yanks a flask from his back pocket and takes a swig. He hands it to Stryder, who passes it to Misty, and before I know it we've all taken a shot of vodka. Gross. It burns like a trail of acid down my throat and straight to my stomach.

"Straight to the Roxie Club," Stryder says to the driver.

I look around, panicked. "You guys can't go to Roxie. We have a six a.m. call time."

Hedge throws me a look telling me I'm crazy. "We can, and we will. Didn't you see us kill it out there? Now, we celebrate!"

Stryder and Misty laugh. Even Derrick is smiling. Wolf is just staring at me. "Why do we have to leave at six tomorrow, anyway?" Wolf asks.

I hesitate to respond. There's no reason, exactly, except to stay on the schedule I created, which minimizes our risk of a late arrival to the venue on Friday. So I cave. "We can push it a couple of hours; that's all. I'm not your babysitter, but I will be a bitch if we're any later than nine."

Wolf chuckles, and everyone else joins in.

"We'll be fine," Derrick says. And for some reason, his words breathe some comfort into my lungs. "You should come, too."

"Count me out," Crawley says from the back seat even though no one was talking to him. And no one tries to persuade him otherwise.

I shake my head. "Not tonight, guys."

Wolf looks at me for a second and then leans in. "I think you should come with me."

With me. Those are the words that echo through my mind, seconds after he's done speaking. My mouth parts, feeling the heat of his words rush through me. I know he didn't mean it that way. Or did he? It doesn't matter.

"It's already late. I can't go out partying with you guys. You forget I have a job to do."

"You should be having fun with us," he says devilishly as a hand skims my thigh, "and I want you to come." There's a gleam in his eyes at the last word, answering my question.

I've been surprised the last few days. Wolf has behaved himself by not once making a move. There's definite flirtation between us, but I've chalked it up to our personalities. It's nice having someone to shoot the shit with. No pressure. No expectations.

I narrow my eyes. "You want me to sit around watching you hit on the locals all night?" I know it's only a matter of time before I witness one of his sexcapades.

"No, I want you to drink, dance, smile, and laugh. I'll hit on *you* if it will make you feel better." He laughs at his own joke. "Just come hang out with us for a little bit. If you want to leave, I'll make sure you get back to the hotel safely."

"Fine," I say with narrowed eyes. "But I want to change first."

"Deal."

"And don't make me regret it."

His smile grows wide in victory. "No promises."

A flutter of nerves alight in my chest when I steal an extra-long glance at his long-lashed, caramel eyes.

Shit.

♪ ♪ ♪

Wolf surprises me, once again. The moment we arrive, I expect fans to be on the ready, flocking to him and battling it out for first dibs. Frankly, I'm curious how he does it. Do they just start lining up, or does he give them the wink and nod to let them know he's interested?

Tonight is a tequila night, which means it's going to get a little crazy around here. I toss back a shot and suck the slice of lime from Lorraine's lips, causing the guys to howl and cheer around us. Not just the band, but everyone who managed to find a way into our little VIP lounge, stocked with white leather couches and a private bar in the corner of the room. A dancefloor takes up most of the space in the center, and there's a bigger dancefloor downstairs that's loud and packed.

The merch team and some of the road crew have joined us, which is cool. I already hope this becomes a thing—once in a while. By my lively chatter and laughter, I know the alcohol is hitting me quickly. It's been a long time since I've let myself feel drunk. I forgot how much fun it is to just let go.

Melanie, who looks hot with her death-defying strappy heels, short leather skirt, and bright yellow strapless top, is becoming a fast friend as we trade ex-boyfriend stories and pop culture gossip. I'm sure I'm divulging far too much information about Tony and Joanna, but the tequila helps reduce all the flying fucks I give.

I'm standing near the couch, dangerously close to Wolf. When I reach over him to set my drink down on the table, he takes the opportunity to grip me by my waist and pull me beside him on the couch. His arm snakes around my shoulders, and he grins before burying his nose in my hair. "You're sexy as sin, you know that?"

We've both had far too much to drink by this point, but I'm alert enough to know I can't take the compliment to heart. I smile anyway. It's hard not to in Wolf's presence. "Thanks."

His nose runs a line from my ear down my neck, and then he presses his lips into the soft spot at its base. I try to ignore the shiver that ripples through me, laughing instead as I try to push him away.

"Where are you going? Sit down," he says with a growl, reaching for me as I finally break free and stand. I'm too quick, stepping back and smiling down at him. His eyes move to my bare legs. My short denim skirt is frayed at the bottom, giving him just enough of a show without revealing all my lady parts.

He frowns and falls back against the couch, squeezing his eyes shut in frustration. Three drinks ago I wouldn't have even considered letting him touch me. God knows I've thought a lot about Wolf's hands and the many places I want them. But if Wolf is going to make a move on me, I'd prefer it be when he's fully coherent. I guess I'm sober enough to make some smart decisions.

"I'm calling for our ride. We really should go."

His jaw clenches and he shakes his head. "We just got here."

I laugh when he tries to reach for me. "Wolf, c'mon. You'll thank me tomorrow."

He pouts and as much as I want to give in to him, I know it's better for us all if I get us out of here. I walk away, noticing now that the VIP area is starting to crowd, and I know the gut instinct I have to leave is the right one.

There's a door near the bar that leads to where we snuck in to avoid the crowd. I leave the same way we came in and jog down the stairs. I check to see if our driver is still outside and see him smoking a cigarette on the brick exterior of the building.

"Hey, Damion," I say. "I'm rounding up the guys, and we should be down soon."

"Yes, ma'am. I'll be ready." He nods, tosses his cigarette to the ground, and stomps it out.

I head back inside, up the stairs, and through the back VIP entrance. The crowd has grown thick fast. I have to squeeze my way through to where the majority of our group is, but the moment I come into view of the couch where I left Wolf, my excitement from the night dissolves.

I'm now faced with the sight of a familiar beauty with bright red hair straddling Wolf, grinding on him like they're alone and not surrounded by thirty people. Rachel's smiling seductively, and my stomach flops like a fish trapped on dry land. He's saying something to her, smiling and gripping her waist, and the band and crew are around them cheering. That's when she leans in and plants her lips on his.

My stomach drops. I've seen enough.

Before I do something stupid like when I found him with Jenn, I walk away.

Lorraine slips through the crowd, throwing her arm around my shoulders. "What's up, sexy?"

I force out a laugh. "Time to go. I'm rounding everyone up. Can you help me?"

Lorraine looks back toward our section and frowns. "Wolf looks busy. I'll stay with Rex and make sure he gets to the hotel okay. I've done this before. You get the other boys."

Part of me wants to resist this idea until I realize it's because I don't want Wolf to go home with anyone but me. This tour is far too long for me to begin thinking like this.

"Sounds good."

I find Derrick, Stryder, Hedge, and Misty. Melanie rounds up her crew, and we head back to the hotel.

I strip naked the moment I get to my room, too tired and drunk to change into something else. Sleep. That will fix everything. There's no way I would be feeling jealous if I wasn't intoxicated … and if Wolf hadn't smelled so damn good when he was kissing my neck.

117

I hate him.

After a few minutes of tossing and turning, I'm finally able to relax and let sleep start to carry me away. But before sleep can completely consume me, a commotion at my door startles me awake.

"It's my room!" insists a drunken Wolf a little too loudly for this time of night. I hear a muffled voice arguing with him and then a click before light from the hallway streams into my room.

What the—?

I hold my breath as he stumbles inside and comes into view, but only slightly. The room is mostly dark again except for a thin strip of light coming through an opening in the curtains.

Wolf makes it to my bed and sits down at the edge. His hands brush through my hair and he strokes my cheeks. "Lyric," he whispers.

I slam my eyes shut, my heart thumping loudly. What the hell is going on right now? I'm torn between wanting him in my room and needing him to leave. It hasn't been that long since I left the club. Where's Rachel?

I let out a ragged breath when his hand brushes across my bare chest. "Fuck, you're naked."

I make no move to pull up the sheet. Air leaves my mouth in staggered breaths, each one pressing my breast into Wolf's palm, and then my eyes flicker to his. His lashes flutter slightly when he releases a breath of his own, and then he tentatively begins to stroke my nipple, his thumb circling it as if silently asking for permission. I know I should speak up now, object to whatever he's about to do to me, but I absolutely want this.

He looks back at my bare chest, swallows, and slides the sheet down until it's below my waist. His fingertips brush the top of my thighs and move up my belly. He pauses at my breasts, then takes a handful into his palm and squeezes. I moan. It's been so long since anyone's touched me like this. Slowly. Tenderly.

I feel a pinch as he tweaks my nipple and then a zing of heat straight between my legs as he lowers his mouth to hover over my breast, his breath sweet and warm as I anticipate his touch. My legs open instinctively to invite him closer, and he moves in a rush, planting himself right where I need him.

Fuck, his jeans. I want to rip them off, but I'm too afraid to move. Too afraid he might disappear. So I cling to his shoulders instead, digging my nails in as a tongue sweeps over one breast, just barely tasting it.

Our breaths escape us in heavy pants, filling the room with a cloud of heat and need.

"You're so fucking sexy," he rasps as his mouth journeys from my chest to my neck, until he's only a hair from my mouth. I've wanted to kiss Wolf since that first day in the elevator, when he said my name like he was making love to it. And now would be a great time to make that happen … but I'm distracted by his hand, which is slowly sliding between my legs.

I move beneath him eagerly, nearly begging him with the buck of my hips. He chuckles with his signature tone, deep with honesty, rich with confidence, and raspy with want.

How is this happening?

We're drunk. For that reason alone I know should stop this, but I don't want to … and I'm convinced that pretending to not want this is just as bad as wanting it. But when his hand moves below my waist and a finger glides against my wet slit, I know it's too late to do anything right. Every inch of my body is screaming for more. And he gives me more when he presses his thumb on my clit before moving it in gentle circles.

"Tell me you want this," he commands.

I don't have the strength to respond with words, so I grip his shoulders tighter. He smiles. I'm acutely aware of his movements, and I can feel his hard-on digging into my leg. He wants me as much as I want him.

Wolf holds my eyes, as if in a challenge, and then he dips one finger in, sinking deep, and then sliding out to add a second finger. I swear his eyes roll back in his head as my tightness squeezes around him.

"I've been wanting to fuck you since you barged into that elevator," he says gruffly. "My fingers are made for you, too. Feel that?"

I let out a strangled cry in response. "Yes," I breathe.

He moves achingly slow, pumping his fingers, never taking his eyes off my face. He leans down and I feel his breath linger over my neck for just a moment before he plants soft kisses on my skin. I sigh at the sweet and commanding combination.

"Let go for me, baby." His voice floats over me. I'm in such a daze, my body buzzing with warning, that I almost miss his request.

"Hmm." My voice is strangled, too distracted by his sexy hands and mouth that deliver such beautiful torture.

He buries his mouth in my neck again and bites down. I gasp. His hot breath begins to tickle my thoroughly teased skin, and that's when the buzz starts to spread. As if he can read my body perfectly, his pumping grows faster and my muscles react, contracting slowly, intensely.

"Wolf," I whisper in warning.

"I've got you." He already knows. The speed of his movements increases, plunging and twisting and flicking until I'm begging for release. "Come for me."

At his command, the surge running through me reaches its climax and bursts brightly. One big wave moves through me, followed by smaller ripples and I convulse for what seems like eternity. I reach for his hand, never wanting this feeling to end, shoving him deeper into me and locking his hand there as I thrust with my hips. I allow every sensation to take over, using his thick fingers for every inch of my release.

When my body relaxes, he growls and slides down my slick skin until his face rests between my legs. His mouth is on me, sampling his first taste before his experienced tongue dips and flicks until my eyes burst open in surprise.

Holy fuck.

Wolf isn't as gentle with his mouth as he was with his fingers. He's consuming me like he's just found water after being stranded in the desert for days. And then his fingers are back inside of me, this time on a furious mission to bring me to my ultimate climax.

I think I'm going to burst as the buzz starts back up again. He's like the Energizer Bunny of oral sex. His head is feverishly moving—as if he's conducting a symphony and his tongue is the master. My body is his orchestra. This time when I convulse around him, he's drinking me dry until he's drained everything that once existed inside of me. Sensibility included.

♪ ♪ ♪

I wake up dripping wet, my fingers inside me, desperate pants infiltrating the air of my hotel room. I'm naked and alone, but fuck, I don't feel alone. Vivid dreams of Wolf making me come multiple times are heavy on my mind as I bring myself to climax. I'm panting when it's all over and cursing my fucked-up mind for wanting it to be him shoving his fingers into me. Especially because Wolf was busy giving someone else orgasms last night.

After a long shower, I dress and throw last night's clothes into my overnight bag. Slinging it over my shoulder, I head down to the breakfast bar before boarding the bus. We still have an hour before we need to be on our way, but I don't want to risk seeing Wolf's face this morning. Not only because he starred as the come-giver of my dreams last night, but because of what I witnessed as I was leaving the bar. I'm not sure why it surprised me. It's what I expected to see when I signed up for this job. But maybe my expectations have changed. I don't know, and I don't want to fucking care.

I shoot a quick text message to the team, hoping it's enough to wake their asses up. Then I grab some coffee and a banana from the buffet, dart outside to the bus, and slip into my bunk. The bottom one that's furthest from Wolf's den. The one that's safest.

As the guys start piling onto the bus, I hear Crawley's heavy steps moving up the aisle. I know he'll want to see my face, so when he nears my bunk, I pull open the curtain and smile. He nods and turns back around, satisfied. I slide the curtain closed again and lie back on my pillow, already knowing I'll be hiding most of the way to Hampton, Virginia.

Just as I'm getting comfortable, my curtain is rudely tugged open, revealing the one face I am in no mood to see. Especially this early in the morning after I spent the wee hours giving myself amazing orgasms to thoughts of him. My cheeks immediately heat under his gaze. His expression is haunted, and I know he wants to say something. But what? Does he want to apologize for getting it on with that rocker skank, Rachel? No apology needed. I have no claim on Wolf, and last night was confirmation as to why that's not something I should ever want.

"Where'd you go last night? I thought we were riding back to the hotel together."

I assume a blank expression as I look back at him. He regrets something—it's all over his face—but I don't want to know what. "Lorraine said she'd see you home. You were busy with a different kind of ride."

I shouldn't have said that. He'll know I care. I don't want to care.

His face falls. "Lyric, nothing happened."

I laugh almost deliriously and turn my stare to the ceiling of my bunk. "It doesn't matter, Wolf. You don't have to explain anything to me."

There's silence as Wolf stares at me. I can feel his eyes burning a hole in the side of my face, but I won't give him anything more.

"Shit," he says, seething. Then he yanks the curtain closed.

He walks away.

A door slams.
My heart sinks.
What the hell was that?

Chapter Eleven

Wolf

Nothing happened with that girl at the club, but that's not why I'm pissed. I'm pissed that I found myself trying to explain to Lyric what really happened. Since when did I let myself get so worked up over a woman? Never. Not even when I was a punk teen who pretended to be a hard-ass to impress girls.

When Lorraine said Lyric took off without me last night, I knew immediately that Rex hadn't gotten Rachel off me in time. I knew Lyric saw, but she saw wrong. I was practically molested by our backstage assistant, and my own drunk ass couldn't control her. This, under normal pre-Lyric circumstances, would have been fine.

I may have been lit, but I know Rachel was all over me, dry humping me in front of my band and crew and whoever-the-fuck else was back there with us. Lorraine joked about it the entire ride home, but I didn't find it funny. I only had one thing on my mind, and her name is Lyric.

I went straight to her room and banged on her door, but she must have already fallen asleep. No one would let me in, so I finally went to bed.

Why am I so concerned about what Lyric saw? Or what Lyric felt when she saw what she did? Why do I feel this insatiable need to protect her as if she were mine? Why do I feel like she *is* mine? She's the furthest thing from it, but that doesn't change the fact that I want to bury myself inside her every time I see her.

There's only one thing I can do on an eight-hour bus ride. If I can't get my mind off Lyric, I'll write my own.

Stay

Emotions blister, feelings fester
Beneath cold skin
You weren't invited in
Your heart is puckered at the surface
Feathers ruffled, you're so damn careless

Strange vibrations, impure intentions
Everything I fear
Our connection so clear
It's the ultimate crime, these sensations I feel
It's every damn thing I fear

Stay … stay away
You're crawling beneath my skin
We're putting a stop to something
Before it ever begins
Just stay … stay away from me

It's missing a bridge and maybe another verse, but I need to get up and stretch. I've been staring at my notebook for hours, unable to keep the words from spilling onto the page. I put the lyrics away and leave the space of my room. Writing never takes a toll on me like this. But then again, my songs are usually about partying and one-night stands. Not infiltrations of the heart.

I let out an amused laugh. If my dad were here right now, he'd tell me I was being a pussy. He'd encourage me to fuck the next chick I laid eyes on hard and fast to get Lyric off my brain. And as much as I detest the man, he'd be right in this case.

Befriending Lyric was a mistake. She's our road manager, and she's got an engrained distrust for rock stars. Maybe a small part of me wanted to prove her wrong. Maybe for a short time I did prove her wrong, but any progress I'd made was shattered last night.

The guys and Lorraine are watching television when I join them in the main living space. Lyric is nowhere to be found. I breathe a sigh of relief, ignoring the dullness in my chest at the thought of her. I want to pound on it until it kick-starts back to life—to the way things used to be, when I didn't obsess over how someone viewed me or interpreted my actions. I need to get over this shit. Because *this* isn't me.

I reach into the refrigerator for a water, ready to wash down the frustration. When I peer above the door, I stiffen. The curtain to Lyric's bunk is opened slightly, just enough to see her sleeping comfortably on a bright blue pillow. At least she looks comfortable. The soft features of her face and those long eyelashes make my heart beat a little faster. I've watched her sleep before. She's kind of beautiful when she sleeps—and she makes these adorable fucking noises.

"Hey, Wolf."

I jump, splashing water down my shirt. "Shit." I close the refrigerator and set the plastic bottle on the counter.

"Check out this riff for 'Dangerous Heart,'" Stryder hollers from the couch, completely missing my blunder. He starts strumming something before I can respond.

I walk over and sit across from him, listening intently and trying to get a feel for it. He repeats it a few times, and then I'm singing along with him.

Can't rely on second chances
Since the first ripped my heart apart
You're not welcome here anymore
Cause there's no going back to the start

"Yeah, man. That's the shit right there." I'm nodding and making him play it again so I can get the vocals right. Lorraine plays a few keys on her portable keyboard, and I smile over at her, loving that we can do this. Jam like this at a moment's notice. It's not long before Derrick grabs his sticks and tinkers around with his beats, and Hedge joins in with backup vocals because his bass is tucked away in the luggage bay.

Over the past few weeks, the band has been working the social media outlets, sharing the video and recruiting help from our fans, searching for the owner of the song. We're up to 15 million hits on YouTube, and radio stations are already calling our label rep, asking for the song.

"What are we going to do if we don't find the writer of this song?" Lorraine asks, disappointment evident in her tone. She's probably the most in love with it—other than me.

The rest of them chime in. Crawley's eyes are on me from the passenger seat of the bus. He's the only one who knows Lyric wrote it. I confided in him the next afternoon and asked him to keep it a secret. I didn't have a choice if I wanted to do things legally. He happily obliged to handle all the legalities. Of course. And we agreed I should be the one to tell the band that we found her, although they would never know who *she* is.

"I've already found her."

"What?" They're all screaming at my confession, causing me to laugh.

"Who the fuck is she? You've been holding out on us?" Hedge glares at me.

"She wants to remain anonymous. Sorry, guys. I can't tell you who she is, but she is letting us keep the song."

"She doesn't want money?" Derrick asks suspiciously.

I shake my head, just as bewildered as the rest of them. "She wants nothing but her anonymity."

The bus gets rowdy, and before I know it, Stryder's passing shots of whiskey around like it's someone's birthday. The jam session continues, and I almost forget that Lyric's asleep in her bunk beside us. I'm not surprised when she wakes up and stumbles groggily into the wild party taking place.

I try to meet her eye, but she avoids me and sits beside Derrick. "What's going on?" she asks him.

A pang of jealousy hits my chest as I watch their exchange and wish she had come to me. Sat by me. "Wolf found the writer of that new song. It's ours. We're celebrating."

Her face tightens, and she immediately stands. "Count me out. I didn't get much sleep last night, and I need to get some work done. See you guys."

She starts to crawl back into her bunk, but I reach her first. "If you need to work you can use my room. It's quiet back there. These guys will probably be rowdy the rest of the trip. They're pumped about the song."

Lyric gives me a half smile. I think she's excited about the song, too, but she's still pissed off about last night. I can't blame her. I'm pissed at myself for last night, and as much as I could lay it all out there and tell her what I'm really feeling, it doesn't change who we are. She doesn't date guys like me, and I don't date women like her.

So then why is Lyric's smile enough to lift me above the clouds?

"Okay, thank you."

I watch her walk away because I can't exactly follow her to my room. Instead, I pick up the keyboard and mess around while Lorraine sings. She has a decent voice and sings backup on some of our songs, bringing a velvety softness to our usually deep-gutted raspy tone.

Derrick is the first to call our impromptu practice session quits when he gets a text message and slips into his bunk. Lorraine and Hedge turn on the PS4, and Stryder carries Misty to his bunk.

Without hesitation, I sneak back to my room and tap the door lightly before entering.

Lyric looks up. She's lying flat on her stomach on my bed, her computer in front of her. She moves to sit up, and I wave my hand. "I'm just going to shower. You can stay."

"I should go," she says, avoiding my eyes.

"I wouldn't go out there," I warn. "Stryder and Misty get loud sometimes. Unless you're into that shit, you should stay. I'll be in here." I point to the door to my bathroom.

"Don't worry." With a final curl of my lip, I step into the tiny bathroom and close the door before leaning against it with a heavy sigh. My heart is pounding.

What the hell is wrong with me? I've never had to work so hard to keep a woman in my company before, but I don't want Lyric to leave. Why am I even trying? Nothing good can come out of this.

Maybe I'll feel better after we clear the air. It's obvious we're attracted to each other, but we both know anything more would complicate our worlds. Neither of us needs that kind of distraction.

Speaking of distractions... It's hard—literally—to keep my mind off the fact that Lyric is lying on my bed right now with her tits pressed into my mattress. Her tight, round ass in the air. Her plush lips pursed as she works.

My hand instinctively finds my cock and begins stroking it as I start the shower. I need to take care of this problem if I'm going to spend any time around Lyric. There are no stops until we hit Pittsburg tonight. Then it's late soundcheck, followed by showtime.

Just the thought of being on stage makes my heart rate speed up, causing my hand to work myself faster. A deep groan slips from my lips. Fuck. What if she heard that?

The last thing I want is for Lyric to freak out and leave to the sound of me jerking off. To thoughts of her.

I release my hardness with a silent cry and squeeze my eyes shut, thinking of anything to make the blood rush simmer. It takes a few minutes and a downpour of cold water, but I'm determined to make it through this shower without imagining Lyric moaning my name.

Still dripping wet, I wrap a towel around my waist and step into my bedroom. I'm expecting to find Lyric there. Still on my bed. Waiting for me. I'm already getting hard again thinking about it.

But she's gone.

My heart starts beating erratically in my chest. I was hoping we could talk. I have no idea what I would have said to her if we got the chance, all I know is that I want that chance fucking desperately.

Looking down at the bulge in the towel, I see my standing ovation demanding attention. Again. "Shit, you're needy today." I rip off the towel and take hold of the rapidly growing purple monster.

Knowing this might take some time, I lean against the wall and close my eyes, thinking of Lyric again. My heart rate quickens with each movement as I imagine her petite, yet strong, hand wrapped around me, her pretty eyes batting up at mine before she takes a mouthful, moving down my shaft until it hits the back of her throat. She's the perfect size to take against the wall, too, or a door, or the glass of a shower. "Ah," I groan as I feel the rush of blood pumping through me.

"Oh my God!"

The sound yanks me from my daydream and my eyes fly open, my hand still wrapped around my beast of an erection. Lyric is in my room, the door closed behind her as if she looked up too late. She doesn't see that I'm staring back at her because her eyes are nowhere near my face.

What the hell do I do now?

She drops the notebook in her hand and backs up against the door, her eyes glued to every movement of my hand. I never stopped stroking myself. No way. She's going to see what she's doing to me. How much I want her.

A grunt escapes my throat as my balls tighten, begging for the release. I reach for them with my other hand and tug. Maybe this won't take as long as I thought. With Lyric standing in front of me, frozen and practically salivating, I make my strokes extra dramatic.

My abs begin to tighten, my head feels like it's ready to explode, and I'm grunting as I release my buildup onto the towel at my feet. I can't remember ever being this turned on before.

"Holy shit," she breathes.

I want to ask her if she enjoyed herself, but I need a moment to catch my breath and let the blood flow start circulating in my body first.

"Was that show for me?" Her unfaltering demeanor shocks me. She finally raises her eyes to meet mine.

"I didn't know you were going to barge in. You could have knocked. Or left. You loved every fucking minute of it."

I'm still breathing heavily. Masturbating in front of a woman isn't a new thing for me, but somehow what I just did gave me the biggest rush. And she's still here, narrowing those pretty eyes at me.

"You were right. Stryder and his girl are loud. I was coming back to wait it out, but I guess I'm not safe anywhere I go, now, am I?" A smirk appears on her face, building my confidence.

"Small bus, big problems." I laugh.

She rolls her eyes, and I don't blame her. That was cheesy as shit, but I don't care.

"You can cover up now. I was going to do some writing."

I reach for my towel, suddenly self-conscious, as she makes herself comfortable on my bed. I wash my hands and throw on shorts before she can get a look at my returning erection. *Fuck*. Not again. I have a problem, and it's clear her name is Lyric. Just one look at her, and my dick reacts as if he's never seen a woman before.

She lies flat on her stomach at the head of my bed, kicking her feet in the air. I join her, propping myself against the headrest, taking in the thin cloth that covers her ass. Barely. My gaze focuses on the crease between her legs and her cheeks.

She glances over her shoulder, and her light green eyes lock on mine. She's smiling, looking sexy as sin with a thin strand of hair falling into her eyes. "What are you looking at?" she asks.

"You."

"Why?"

"Because I'm picturing you naked. Only fair. You just saw me in all my glory."

She laughs. "Not my fault." Turning back to her notebook she mumbles. "It was one hell of a show."

My chest puffs with excitement. Damn straight.

"So," she says casually, "everyone's stoked about the song, huh?"

I knew she cared.

"Yup. It'd be cooler if they knew who wrote it. They already have mad respect for you, but this would blow their minds."

The blush that creeps up her cheeks tells me just knowing that is enough for her.

"So, what is it with you and that song?" I prod. "Are you ever going to tell me?"

Her cheeks darken before a thick curtain of hair falls over her shoulder, shielding me from catching any more hints in her expression. "It's just ... the pressure. Having music legends for parents didn't make life easy. I always felt like I was disappointing someone, you know? Because I was never going to be a musician. But I loved the industry. I always felt a little lost and without anyone there to guide me..." she shrugs. "I wrote lyrics."

"Did your parents know?"

She's silent for a long time before answering. "Yeah, they knew."

"So, what? You were afraid your lyrics weren't good enough? I'm sure you've gotten better since then. Or maybe you just needed to get your songs in front of someone who needed them. Like me."

Lyric flips her long brown hair over her shoulder and smiles back at me. "You think you have me all figured out."

I let out a breath of air. "Actually no. I don't. Not at all." *And it's bothering the hell out of me.*

Her feet sway slightly in the air, so I instinctively reach for the closest one and pull it to my lap. When I do, the fabric of her shorts leg stretches open at the center, revealing shimmering pink flesh. She's not wearing any underwear.

"I didn't fuck Rachel last night," I blurt out.

"Wolf," she says, her voice low with warning.

"She was crawling all over me, but I didn't touch her except to yank her off. When Rex removed her, you were already gone. I wanted to ride back with you. You fucking left. You could have said something to me."

I'm not sure if it's the situation from last night or the sight of her bare beneath those shorts that's firing me up, but before I know it, my hand is working her foot like I should be working my hard dick right now.

"What are you doing?" It comes out as a croak as she shakes her foot in my lap, but I hold onto it and press my fingers into her arch. When she lets out a little groan, my cock jumps in my lap.

I'm still staring at her naked flesh, which causes my strokes to quicken. She lays her head down, giving up on her notebook and sighing. She has no idea what she's doing to me with every innocent sound that comes out of her mouth. I'm not sure how to stop touching her, or watching her, or imagining placing myself between her tight ass cheeks.

I clear my throat, coming to a decision. "I think you should let me fuck you."

Everything about her freezes, and I'm not sure if she's considering it or if she's ready to lunge off the bed and into the other room. She turns her head to assess me, to see if I'm serious. I'm dead serious.

This is it! The answer to our problem. We fuck. We get it over with. A one night stand. I show her how well it can work, and we get it out of our system. Then we go back to business as usual.

"Let's not be shy about this, Lyric. You're insanely attractive, and while fooling around is probably the last thing we should be doing, I want to so damn bad." I swallow, hoping I'm making a good case. "Just once."

My fingers move up her ankles slowly. She twitches a little but makes no move to stop me. I continue the journey up her calves, then her hamstrings, and then to the bottom of her glutes, where the thin fabric of her shorts ends. The room is silent except for the sound of her harsh breaths and my own heart beating down the walls of my chest.

She's still as a board, her eyelids pressed tightly together. I consider removing my hand altogether to give her a chance to decide before my fingers take off on a mission determined by the thickness between my legs. My poor dick is throbbing.

When she shifts a little, I know she's giving me permission, but I hesitate. Lyric isn't a rocker slut. She's so much more, and she deserves so much more. More than I could probably ever give her.

But she wants this. *Me.* Maybe she needs a release just like I do.

Letting out a ragged breath, I slip my finger beneath the fabric of her shorts until it meets her pussy. So perfect. So wet. Already.

Fuck.

I glide my finger up and then down at a tortuously slow pace, giving her every chance in the world to refuse me. Her legs slide open, her clit swollen beneath my touch. I still make no move to take the plunge, not yet, although I know it's what she wants.

I let her shift a bit more. She's practically begging for it, and it's hot as hell, but if this is really happening, I'm going to make it last as long as possible. Lyric deserves the VIP treatment. Multiple orgasms initiated by intense and mind-blowing foreplay. She'll be screaming when she comes in my mouth, but only when I'm ready to let her.

My finger slips back down her leg, drawing a wet line down her skin. Reaching for the band of her shorts, I swiftly remove them, revealing the finest ass I've ever seen. It's round and firm, sitting perfectly below her tiny waist.

Just staring at Lyric's curves is enough to get me off. Seeing her bare is more arousing than I was ready for. I pull my erection from my shorts and tug at it a few times, hoping to relieve some of the pressure. To my surprise, Lyric takes that moment to look at me over her shoulder, her eyes darkening by the second. I squeeze her ass and watch as her teeth sink into her plush bottom lip. I fucking lose it.

I shift her so her legs are on either side of mine and my feet are angled to lock her body in place. She's still lying flat on her stomach and I'm still sitting with my back resting against the headboard, but now her clit is directly below my cock. Right where I want it. With her eyes still on me, I stick a finger in my mouth and suck, giving her an idea of what I'm about to do. I grin and sink it straight into her wet opening until her eyes roll back in her head.

Hell yes. So warm and soft, but tight. So tight. My dick throbs knowing those narrow walls will be wrapped around me soon. I don't know if I can resist much longer. Not after knowing what's waiting for me.

My free hand palms one of her ass cheeks, gripping it for leverage as I sink and twist and jerk my finger in her depths. My hands are big, and one finger is enough for someone as tight as Lyric, but if I'm going to prepare her for taking all of me when I'm ready to give it, she needs to understand what she's in for. So I dip a second finger into her tightness ... and then a third. She screams a little. It's a quiet scream, but a scream no less. I smile in victory while continuing to pump until her walls begin to strangle me. She's so close.

Call me a savage beast, but I won't let her come yet. That was just a primer. I release my fingers while she mewls in disappointment.

I'm quick to maneuver her to the foot of the bed until her head and arms dangle off, and then I move to my knees and lift her legs until they're propped up on my shoulders.

Then she's in my mouth. There's no mercy now. No gentleness. Pure mouth-fucking, and it's beautiful. Her pussy is perfection and her juices are sweet, just as expected. I suck her clit, already knowing the pressure she needs to send her into a state of orgasm. She chases a moan with a scream until she's convulsing wildly against my face. She comes for what seems like minutes as I continue my work on her.

"Jesus, Wolf," she says through deep, heaving breaths, her first words since asking me what I was doing.

I chuckle into her wet heat, flip her body, and pull her closer so her head rests on the foot of the bed. I leave her for only a second to remove my shorts, and then I climb back onto the bed, my dick angry as hell at me for taking so long. "Please tell me you're on birth control," I moan, brushing the crown of my cock against her pussy.

Her eyes are glazed over when she peers back at me. It's all cute until she opens her mouth to respond, and I know her answer isn't going to be a good one. It's like someone kicked my puppy when she shakes her head. "I stopped taking it. Do you have protection?" She looks almost as sad as I am.

Fuck. Fuck. Fuck. I shake my head. "No."

Why didn't I think of that before getting on this bus? Lyric and all her distractions, that's why. For the first time in years, my goal wasn't to fuck as many women as possible on the road.

I still consider shoving my cock into her before she can resist me. I need to be inside her now. I've waited patiently, and I finally have my chance. Rubbing the head of my dick against her again, I moan, but I think I might cry.

"I can pull out." It's worth a shot.

She shakes her head firmly. "No."

"I'll ask one of the guys." I make a move to get up, but she grabs my arm.

"You can't do that," she whispers. "They can't know."

I growl and let my head fall into her neck. "Baby, I *need* to get inside you. You have no idea how many times I've thought about fucking your sweet pussy. If this doesn't happen, I swear my dick is going to fall off."

She giggles, and even in my state, I smile at the sound. "We can do something else," she says coyly.

I raise an eyebrow, wondering if a blow job will suffice.

"Do you have any oil or lotion?"

"Hell yeah, I do." I hop off the bed to grab a bottle of edible lube from my bathroom. I'm heaving quick breaths at the thought of taking her ass. When I return, she's slipping her shirt over her head and removing her bra, letting her beautiful tits out to play.

Why didn't I get those in my mouth earlier?

"You're so hot, babe." I can't help moving my eyes across her body, appreciating. She smiles before taking the bottle from me and squeezing a string of clear liquid onto her chest. I begin stroking myself as I watch her, promising my balls their release soon.

I think I'm going to come before I even touch her again. When she's done spreading the oil all over her breasts, I practically run to the bed and straddle her. It's a slippery journey for my hands as they glide up her ribcage and over her tits. I lick each one, silently apologizing for not tending to them sooner.

She giggles at my obvious distraction and lies back on the bed. It finally dawns on me what she wants me to do. Taking her full breasts in her hands, she holds them together, using her thumbs to rub her nipples slowly. I admire her confidence and the perfect curves of her body before allowing my cock to slip into position. I growl when she squeezes her plump breasts against me, hugging my length tightly.

It's like I've died and gone to heaven when I start to move. Lyric's tits are big for a petite girl, but they aren't fake. I can't remember the last time I fucked real boobs. These feel better as they conform willingly to every inch of me.

The fact that I see so much of Lyric as I'm titty fucking her—and she sees so much of me—is causing a shortage in my brain. So many women over the years, and this is the one I want to turn the lights on for. This is the woman I want to see, even when I close my eyes.

Sweat drips down my body as I gain momentum. I have the strongest desire to plant my lips on her and feed her the sounds of what she's doing to me.

"Baby, are you ready for me?"

Her eyes light up, and we both shift so I'm no longer between her tits. I'm on my knees while she sits cross-legged, and I'm in her mouth without a single beat lost between us.

It's like we've done this a million times, and no words are necessary to know what the other needs.

One of her hands rests on my ass while the other plays with my balls and holds my cock. This chick will be the death of me. She pulls me deep into the back of her throat. My dick has girth and length, so I don't expect her to take it all, but she does a pretty fucking good job.

"So. Good." I grunt each syllable, articulating, so there's no mistake.

She uses this moment to take more of me, and then her cheeks go hollow as she sucks, detonating the pending explosion. "Ah," I grunt as she strokes every last drop into her waiting mouth in calculated spurts.

When she swallows and licks her lips, I want her again. This is insane. I've come twice in the last hour, but I know it won't take much rest for me to build up again.

I fall back onto the bed, my arms crossed over my eyes. I can't look at her. If I do, I'll want her again and again, until my dick really does fall off.

A moment later, the bed dips, and I force myself to look up. "Where are you going?" I growl.

She slips on her shorts and looks around for something. I can feel her bra digging into my back and look down to see her shirt right next to it. She sees them at the same time and reaches over me. I smile and grip her waist, pulling her onto my chest. "I didn't say you could leave."

Her eyebrows raise, but she's smiling. "I should probably go before your friend gets excited again and we do something stupid."

Her words crush me, but I don't understand why. "Stupid as in have sex?"

Lyric tilts her head. "I'm not having unprotected sex with you, Wolf. The longer we stay in this room together, the probability of that happening gets better."

"Really?" I ask, already starting to get excited.

She cuts me off with her eyes. "Not happening."

I stare back, locking eyes with her, desperately wanting to look deeper. There are so many emotions floating around, camouflaged in specks of gold and glimmers of light. She's fucking beautiful, and I'm not thinking this way because she just drank from my fountain. Usually after I get a woman off and vice versa, I can't wait to send them out the door. No repeats allowed. But not this time. There's an ache in my chest at the thought of her leaving.

"Wolf," she whispers in a silent plea to let her go.

I refuse, tightening my hold around her waist. "Stay. No sex. No finger fucking. I won't even try to lick your pussy again. I can be good."

She groans and laughs at the same time. "This was a one-time thing, remember?"

My face twists with mock confusion. "We didn't even have sex. One-night stands include sex. This isn't over."

Rolling her eyes, she pushes away from me, not even trying to cover her glorious breasts. They're perfect, just like the rest of her. "I'd like to get dressed."

Sighing, I hand her the rest of her clothes and sit up, pressing my feet into the floor. "So that's it?"

She raises a brow. "Yeah, I guess I should say thank you."

Damn, this woman plays hardball. I laugh and shake my head. "You are something else, Lyric Cassidy."

With a wink, she walks toward my door, giving me an over-the-shoulder smile before opening it. "Thanks for the good time, Wolf Chapman." Then she walks out.

And that's where this is supposed to end.

Yeah fucking right.

Chapter Twelve

Lyric

What happened between Wolf and me last week makes everything awkward. Every time I'm forced to be in the same room as him and my eyes happen to slip up and catch his, I remember everything. The way he held my body when I came. His sweet, tentative mouth, on me like a man on a mission.

I don't care if he told me I wasn't his type when we first met. He was full of shit. But how can I trust that he and I could actually be anything more with his reputation and my fear of repeating my same mistakes?

Did I want to walk out of his room that day? Hell no. And that's where all my problems begin. I want to trust that he won't be like the last, so badly I'm almost willing to sacrifice my own heart in the process. This time I'm fighting it with everything in me.

There hasn't been a time when we've been together that he hasn't devoured me with just one look. After striking up an unlikely friendship with him, my own morals must have gone completely out the window. And when I walked in on him masturbating, his eyes closed and fist pumping his erection, I knew he was thinking about me. I should have walked out before he saw me, but I froze, unable to take my eyes off his rock-hard body and his generous length. Even if we'd tried to have sex, I'm certain his size would have been an obstacle. But fuck me, I like a good challenge. If it weren't for our lack of protection, I would have happily exchanged boob sex to have him inside me.

With our forced proximity, there's only so much I can do to stay away from Wolf. What I *cannot* do is handle those tempting caramel eyes and gorgeous smile. Not when they're aimed at me, and especially not when they're aimed at someone else. Wolf is currently carrying a conversation with Natalie Whitman, a hotshot radio producer's daughter with an adoration for Wolf she's made public on numerous counts.

Tonight, we're at a party in New York City hosted by Rockland Radio and Broadcasting Network, home to over three thousand satellite stations. They're a huge reason why Wolf has been so successful ... and Natalie knows this.

She's pretty. That's the first thing I notice. Petite. Auburn hair. A full rack, packaged with class, unlike most other women who are trying to get Wolf's attention. Nothing to hate in the sexy-as-fuck department, as Wolf would say. And he's leaning into her ear, whispering something that makes her blush.

The second thing I notice is how much I care.

My stomach rolls just as it did that night in the club when Rachel straddled him. I haven't been back to a club with the guys since. Instead, every time the boys go out, I convince Melanie, Lorraine, and Misty to find our own bar or curl up together in a hotel room to enjoy the free movie stations, courtesy of Wolf.

For the first time in a long time, I enjoy hanging with a group of girls. We seem to all be here for different reasons. No one's creating drama over men, and our mutual love for eighties movies provides endless entertainment. Not only that, but these girls have been tainted by the industry, too. They aren't victims of the scene. They are the scene.

"You think they'll do it in the bathroom or make it back to the hotel?" Melanie smirks as she watches Natalie lean into Wolf as she laughs.

I snort to cover up my discomfort. "I haven't been witness to one of his conquests yet. I'd rather not start tonight."

Melanie gives me that look—the one that tells me she knows I'm secretly attracted to Wolf—but Jesus Christ, who isn't? Maybe her. I don't know why. Honestly, I'm afraid to ask, because if she's hooked up with Wolf too, that would put us in an awkward situation. I've had enough awkward to last me a while.

I flip around to face the bar my back was just pressed up against. The bartender sees me and nods before heading my way. "Two shots. Whiskey, please."

Melanie and I take our shots and make our way to the other side of the room where Stryder and Misty are chatting. "I think we're going to head back," Misty frowns. "Stryder isn't feeling well and we have a six a.m. wakeup call tomorrow thanks to our whip-cracker road manager."

I grin at the compliment. At least I'm taking it as a compliment. "Good plan. Should I round everyone up first?"

Lorraine nods her head at Wolf and Natalie across the room. "I think Wolf found himself a ride again." She chuckles lightly. "I'll just let him know we're heading out. Lyric, can you find the rest of the guys?"

The thought of leaving Wolf alone with Natalie makes my heart feel heavy in my chest. If I leave and they hook up and I accept the way things are between us, then I only have myself to blame. But it's not like our situation will change. Sure, our chemistry is hot, and his mouth in all the right places will be forever impossible to forget. But there's more to it than that. There's a friendship I thought we'd finally found. I miss it.

I speak before I have time to reconsider my actions. "Why don't you grab everyone else? I need to talk to Wolf before we leave. I'll let him know we're going."

Lorraine nods and walks over to talk to Derrick. I take a step, but Melanie grabs my hand, holding me back. "Wait up a sec," she says quietly. "You know Wolf's like this, right? It's just who he is."

My heart sinks fast and deep into a pit of disappointment. I hate that I'm no longer in control of the anchor. "I'm fine. I don't care, honestly, Mel. I just need to tell him something before we leave." I smile, hoping it's convincing enough. Her smile is pinched when she returns it, and then she walks off with Stryder and Misty.

What the hell am I doing?

As I approach Wolf and Natalie, I notice they're even closer than they were before. His hand is on her waist. Her boobs are pressed against his chest. And they're taking turns speaking, keeping their voices low enough that I can't hear them upon my approach. I clear my throat.

Wolf sees me first, his eyes narrowing and his jaw tightening. "Lyric, what's up?"

I smile at Natalie, hoping she's less afflicted by my intrusion. Her kind smile only makes me feel worse. "I'm sorry, Wolf, can I speak to you for just a minute? Before I take off?" I swallow, hoping that's enough for him to step away from the beautiful woman in his arms.

He hesitates, but follows me a few feet to the edge of the room. "This better be good," he growls lowly.

His anger surprises me, even for him. He's never treated me unkindly, even after our failed attempt at having sex. Heat forms behind my eyes, hating that it's come to this. Hating so much that I care. "I-I'm sorry. It's just … we're leaving, and I want to make sure you get back to the hotel okay."

He's silent, his eyes moving between mine, as if he's waiting for me to elaborate on why I pulled him away. I've got nothing else.

He lets out a puff of breath and leans down, pressing his mouth to my ear. Goose bumps explode across my skin. His voice is low as he speaks.

"I'm just going to put this out there, Lyric, because I'm not one to play games." I hold my breath. "I'm going to take Natalie back to my room tonight, and I'm going to fuck her." I gasp, hating myself for it, but what the hell? "Hard," he adds, as if the first part wasn't enough.

"You don't have to—"

He leans back slightly to look me in the eyes. "Yes, I do have to tell you this. You should know, because you and I both know there's something between us. Something neither of us is willing to explore. So tonight, I'm going to fuck someone else."

"You're doing this because of me?"

He laughs, a throaty laugh that rips my heart in two. "I'm doing this because I haven't had sex in weeks. And there's a hot piece over there who's practically stayed a virgin waiting for one night with me."

There's a burning sensation in my eyes caused by a jealousy so ferocious I could explode. I pray to God he doesn't notice. "You're going to sleep with her and leave her, and you're going to break her heart." *And mine.* My eyes slip from his for just a second when I can feel my voice begin to tremble. "We both know you'll do what you want, so do what you need to do, Wolf. Just don't blame me when it's all over." And that's when a tear slips down my cheek.

He leans in closer so I can feel his cheek just barely scrape mine. "I'm not who you want me to be." His tone is gentle now, apologetic. "I'm not what you need."

I reach out, gripping his waist as another tear falls.

With a stuttered breath, I take his words and accept them, pull away from his warmth, and walk away without looking back.

"I know," I whisper.

♪ ♪ ♪

It's almost two in the morning when I finally give up on sleep and step into the hallway. Relaxing is impossible after the my conversation with Wolf.

He's right. He's a rock star with no commitments. He's been nothing but honest with me since the beginning, and he's done absolutely nothing wrong. It's me that's the fool. It's me who puts up a sheet of ice so thick Wolf couldn't get to know me if he tried. And in his own way, he has tried.

I pull change from my pocket and slip a few quarters into the vending machine before selecting my poison. Snickers always soothes. Then again, I missed dinner. Maybe I should go with something healthier. Rolling my eyes at my own conscience, I press the letter-number combination for Snickers and then move to the soda machine.

"Two a.m. munchies. You're either high, or you're punishing your body for wanting something else you think you can't have."

I flinch, but I don't turn to look at Wolf. I'd know that raspy tone anywhere. I've melted for it. Starved for it. But not anymore. Not after Natalie.

I try to concentrate on my drink selection. I'm in the midst of inserting money into the slot when Wolf's warm body moves behind me, pressing against me. Chest to my shoulders. Hands on my waist. He leans down, his nose falling into my neck, skimming upwards until it reaches my ear. "I'm sorry," he whispers.

My body trembles at the heaviness of his words. They wash over me and seep into my pores before I can attempt to escape them. He's sorry. He's sorry for having sex with another girl? He's sorry for telling me his intentions? None of it heals my heart. A heart that was already bruised to begin with. I'm so over this shit.

I let out a deep breath, punch in my code, and lean over to retrieve my drink. I swivel to face him, ready to tell him to go to hell when I notice what he's wearing. Or better yet, what he's not wearing. I bite my bottom lip as my eyes moving down his bare chest to the navy pajama pants that cling to his muscles. And other things. I finally pull my eyes away in order to clear my head, because *damn*.

"You have nothing to be sorry for," I finally say.

Wolf lets out a breath and rakes his hands through his hair, seeming frustrated. "I didn't have to speak to you like that." He blows out another breath. "It was pretty shitty of me, actually."

I shrug, not knowing what to say to that. He's right. "Okay, well, apology accepted. Have a good night, Wolf." I step around him.

"Wait. I can't sleep either."

My steps halt momentarily as I let out a laugh. "I'm sure you'll figure it out." I take another step to leave, but his hand grips mine before I make any progress. He swivels me around and backs me against the wall. Every inch of his front is pressing against me, and his fingers are threading through mine.

"I'm only going to say this once, and then I'm going to let you go. Okay?"

I nod slowly.

"I didn't fuck anyone tonight." Air freezes in my throat at his words. He's lying. He slept with her and tossed her, and now he feels like shit. But his eyes tell me different, and they're speaking directly to my heart. "It's actually becoming a problem," he continues. "And I'm sorry, but I'm going to start blaming you."

Anger swirls through. "You can't blame me for everything."

He nods slowly, jaw tensing and relaxing steadily. "Oh, yes I can. It's clear as day. Because until you slammed into me on that elevator, my life was pretty fucking easy."

My eyes narrow, appalled that he would think to blame me for his impotence. "Screw you, Wolf."

He smirks. "Baby, that's all I want right now."

I push against him with my hands, but he's a brick wall of resistance. A brick wall that apparently retaliates. He steals my palms from his chest and pins them against the wall. He leans forward until his mouth is hovering above mine. "Don't fucking push me."

My chest tightens and squeezes into my throat. I've shed too many tears over him. I can't cry now. "What do you want, Wolf?" I choke out.

His expression grows softer, his eyes tender as they plead with mine. "I want to kiss your pretty mouth."

I swallow, silently screaming for my tears to stay back. "And then what?" I challenge through my breathy words.

Now it's his turn to smile as he stares at my lips while readying his with a slow sweep of his tongue. "Then I guess we'll see."

His mouth lands on mine, softly at first, deepening when my lips finally part for him. I moan. Something must be wrong with me. I swear, it didn't take a second for me to stop fighting him and kiss him back. Our mouths work together, igniting the same sparks I felt before. The same sparks that could potentially grow into flames of our own making. A fire that will burn us all to the ground if this ends badly. And there's no doubt it's going to end badly.

He grips the backs of my thighs and lifts me. My legs instinctively wrap around his waist until I can feel him pressing into me, our mouths never stopping. My hands move through his hair, gripping tightly and tugging until he groans.

"My room," he growls between kisses. "Now."

Chapter Thirteen

Wolf

"Two for you, one for me," I tease, nipping at Lyric's swollen clit. She jerks at the sensitivity.

"Orgasm ratio? That's really what you're doing right now?"

I grin, feeling lighter than ever. "I'll always make sure you get off more than me."

"Lucky ladies," she spews sarcastically.

Narrowing my eyes at her, I consider her intention behind the words. "I said *you*, Lyric. Just you." I move up the bed, not ready to go into more detail, and lie back, turning on the television.

I flip through the channels, wishing there were ways we could get off together, like, at the same time. Apparently, I have a serious problem with condoms. Turns out the new box I purchased is defective. The moment I slid the first one on, the condom ripped at the head. Several curse words later, I tried another. Same problem. I kept trying until I'd emptied the entire box and chucked all the contents across the room.

Part of me thinks she likes the fact that we haven't had sex yet. She laughs at my frustration. And I love when Lyric laughs, so I play it up a little, exaggerating my pout. Her laugh is like an instrument playing the sweetest, softest melody. It just might be my ultimate weakness.

Neither of us could sleep after we went back to my room last night, so we fooled around instead and grabbed breakfast from the hotel café before sneaking onto the bus. We were the first ones on, so we shut the door to my den, as she likes to call it, and collapsed on my bed. This time, we slept.

Hours later, we woke up and realized the bus was moving, which meant Crawley must have peeked in and saw us wrapped in each other's arms. I don't give a shit. Lyric smells good. Feels good too. All of that is something the old Wolf would have never known. But with Lyric's quiet strength combined with our sexual chemistry, I'm not ready to send her packing.

"Maybe you should forego your room when we get to the hotel today. Stay with me tonight." My eyes are focused on the television while I speak casually. As if what I asked isn't a big fucking deal.

My arms are secured behind my head and Lyric is snuggled up against my bare chest, eyes focused on me. "Really?" She sounds nervous. Maybe she needs more convincing.

"I'm pretty sure I could go through an entire box of condoms tonight if you let me try." I smirk, and she laughs.

"You're such a romantic."

I freeze and turn to look at her. "Is that what you want? Romance? With me?" I might have to contemplate this if it's something Lyric wants. Right now, I can't imagine letting her out of my sight, not even to slip into a room ten feet away.

Lyric's eyes hold her shock, but she releases it with a laugh. "Don't do that. Don't say these things to me in the moment when we both know neither of us can handle a relationship right now."

Is it so bad to think that I could maybe want a relationship with Lyric? Even I seem to think I'll mess this up somehow, but what if I don't? "I'm not promising anything," I agree. "But it's different with you."

Her expression falls, and I desperately wish I could read this woman's mind. "It's just because we haven't had sex yet," she says with a shake of her head.

I want to grab that head, hold it still, and make her stop thinking so damn much.

"Don't worry, Wolf. I won't be *that* girl, okay? I won't ask you for something you've admitted you don't do. I just got out of a relationship, anyway, so I'm not ready for that kind of emotional turbulence."

"With that fuck, Tony? You still messed up over him?"

Lyric shakes her head in frustration. "No, it's not like that. It's not about him. It's about—"

"I know. Rock stars. You think we're all the same."

"Aren't you?" She cries incredulously. "You've said it yourself." She shakes her head, dragging a slow, deep breath between her lips. "Look. I think I'm okay with fooling around. You know, until we call it quits. Maybe at the end of the tour."

A blow below the belt. "What the hell does that mean?" It might make me a hypocrite, but I didn't expect this from Lyric. Not that I had plans for us after fucking. That has always kind of been the end goal, but right now, I don't want anyone else.

My jaw hardens, and I know she sees my expression change because hers does, too. "That's shitty, Lyric." I loosen my grip on her, and she tries to meet my eyes again, but I've already looked away. If she doesn't move off me, I'll move her myself.

"I'm not your type, remember?" Her words come out in a rush. "Isn't this just about sex? I get it, Wolf. You're not secretive about your relationship preferences. You don't have a girlfriend by choice. You're content to bounce from one girl to the next, and while I'll never understand that, I'm smart enough to know I need to shield my heart from you. I have no expectations."

She's not wrong for saying these things, but they still hurt. She wasn't supposed to be like the others. Using me for her own release. In the past, the "using" has always been mutual. Women use me for bragging rights and a good time while I use them for the release I need.

No expectations. What if *I* have expectations? I do. I did. The thought of making Lyric come as many times as possible over the course of this tour came to mind a few times in the last twelve hours. What if I don't want it to end when our tour does? What if I don't want Lyric to shield her heart from me?

Shit.

Realizing I brought this upon myself, I bite back my anger and smile. She's right. I've made it no secret that I'm not the type of guy to be with only one woman. But then why does it feel like she just reached into my chest and squeezed my heart with her small, unsuspecting hands?

"You're a smart girl, Lyric." This time I manage to roll her off me. I stand and pull my shorts on before taking the three steps to my tiny closet to grab a shirt. Without a word, I leave my bedroom, shutting the door behind me. I walk past the bunks and into the living area to join the rest of the guys in front of the television.

Stryder gives me a knowing glance, and he doesn't look happy about it. He probably thinks I've just fucked Lyric and now I'm done with her. I guess in a way I am, but not by choice. Not at all.

Chapter Fourteen

Lyric

My breath left with Wolf when he exited the room, but I know better than to call after him. He played it off like I didn't hurt him, but I saw the pang of emotion in his eyes when I told him I needed to shield my heart from him.

What did he expect? What did he want *me* to expect?

Confusion consumes me as I rush from the bus to the main counter of the hotel in Gilford, New Hampshire to check us in, Crawley trailing behind me. I haven't done shit all afternoon, and I'm going to be sorry for it if anything goes wrong.

After giving George, the man at the front desk, the booking information and my ID, he taps away on his screen. I watch his face change, and my heart sinks as he opens his mouth to speak. "I'm sorry, Miss Cassidy. It looks like your reservation got bumped."

"You've got to be bloody kidding me," Crawley voices under his breath as he walks away, and I grind my teeth in frustration.

"That's impossible," I say, focusing on the man behind the counter. "I have the confirmation right here. Your hotel even requested a deposit and we went ahead and paid in full." I practically throw my phone onto the counter and wait for the damn app to load. My cheeks flame as George stares pityingly at me while the line of anxious hotel guests grows in my shadow.

Crawley is on his phone, pacing at the entrance of the hotel now, I assume trying to find alternate accommodations in case I can't get this mess sorted out.

"Look!" I tap my phone's screen again, revealing the confirmation from the hotel.

The man squints at it while he types something into his computer and then nods. "There's been a mix up, Miss Cassidy. I do apologize. It appears you booked twenty rooms, but we were only able to secure six."

"Six?" I squeak. "How did that happen?"

"You never received a call from us?"

"No." I shake my head violently, trying to remain calm, but it's impossible as I look over my shoulder and see Derrick and Stryder approach Crawley. Crawley says something heatedly and then they all look at me. My face gets flushed all over again.

I turn back to George. "You need to fix this. These arrangements were made well in advance. These are VIP guests who expect to stay in your hotel."

The man nods. "Yes, miss. I'm seeing what we can do now. I apologize for the inconvenience."

The inconvenience. He has no idea.

"Aha," he finally says with a smile. "Another room opened up, so that makes seven rooms for you here. Unfortunately, I do not have any more space, but we have a sister hotel down the street that would be happy to take the remainder of your party."

"Fine." I'm seething. "Just book it, and please provide us with transportation. We've already sent the buses away."

The man gives me no argument, which is smart. He also acts as if his hotel didn't just humiliate me at the worst possible time. I push off the counter and meet Crawley at the door. He pulls his mouth away from the phone and waits expectantly for me to give him good news.

"Seven can stay here. They're providing other accommodations for the rest. Transportation is on its way. I'm so sorry about this, Crawley—"

"Lyric, don't start." His agitated voice runs over me like cold water as his eyes scan the room. No one seems to be paying any attention to us, but he's clearly heated because of my fuck up.

"I'll tell the band they can stay," Crawley says. "Rex and I will stay, too. Ride with the others to the other hotel and email me with room details."

I nod and straighten my posture, then hand him the keycards. *Everything will be fine.* I breathe. "Will do."

Just as I'm turning away, Crawley calls me back. I halt and turn to face his narrowed eyes. A shudder vibrates through me as I wait for his words.

"I hoped you would prove me wrong. You're here for the tour, not Wolf's todger." His voice is low and controlled. "I don't bloody care who your parents are. A mistake like this happens again and I'll see to it that your reputation is permanently fucked." He waves a hand, dismissing me as he walks away.

My jaw drops. There it is. Crawley is officially a dick. It takes all my strength to control my body and mouth from reacting to his ugly words. I may have screwed up by not calling to confirm our reservations again, but I don't deserve that shit.

My stomach is in knots by the time I finally stumble out the door. Wolf is walking into the hotel and slows when he sees me, but I don't stop. I breeze by him to round of the rest of the crew. I can't lose my cool now. Not until I'm safely alone, locked up in my hotel room.

Our shuttle is slow as hell to arrive, but the crew and I finally make it to the sister hotel. No one seems to care about the botched hotel plans but me and Crawley, so I try my best to act like I don't care either. We're already checked in by the time we arrive, and the management passes out our hotel keycards. After listening to a drawn-out apology from the Manager that comes with free future stays, hotel discounts, and as many room upgrades as they could give us, I rush off to my room, ignoring Melanie's pleas to get me to go out tonight. No fucking way.

As soon as I close the door behind me, the sobs heave from my chest. I've never been so embarrassed. I fall into my bed and wrap myself up safely under the comforter. I can't wait for this day to be over.

♪ ♪ ♪

It's just after nine p.m. when Wolf finally calls. I knew he would contact me eventually, but after everything that went on today, I throw my phone across my bed instead of answering it. My eyes are swollen and red from the tears that refused to let up after the hotel room disaster, but that was only salt in the wound. The truth is, I'm really messed up over Wolf.

I have no doubt sex with him would be mind-blowing, but where would that leave us when it's all over? Wolf doesn't do repeats. I've heard it from him and from his bandmates a million times. It's a joke every time a familiar face tries to get close to him. And the thing is, Wolf doesn't give women the wrong impression. He's straightforward with his preference for one-time fucks, and he's never had an inclination for anything else.

I'd be a fool to think I'm any different.

Our flirting was one thing, but when he put his hands on me, that was when it got real. When his finger slid inside me, I knew I never wanted another man's finger to sink into me again. How did my heartbreak over one man so quickly turn into a deep, festering desire for another? My heart should still be healing; instead, it's thriving, and I'm not sure there's anything I can do to stop it.

But then there's Crawley's words. *Crawley*. He can be such a prick. He has some nerve threatening my career. Sure, I should have triple-checked the hotel arrangements before our arrival, something I would have done if I wasn't getting oral stimulation from the lead singer at the time. But in the end, it was the hotel's fuckup. Not mine.

Still, I can't help but feel like a joke to the band now. If any of the guys heard me coming beneath Wolf's magical tongue, I'm officially a rocker slut. And the worst road manager ever. I can see it now. Every fuckup will be attributed to the fact that I let Wolf put his hands on me. It pisses me the hell off. And *that*, above anything else, is why I won't answer his call. That's why I refuse, from here on out, to let him get to me.

Wolf's life was just fine before I came along. He said it himself. From now on, I'm not stepping foot in his bedroom. I don't even think our runs are safe anymore. I'll avoid every room he's in unless it's for official business. I'll kick ass at my job because I'm great at it, and he'll kick ass on stage because he's great at that. He'll have his lineup of girls waiting for him at the next show, so it doesn't matter how I choose to play this. The important thing is that I put my focus into my job instead of the many inches of Wolf.

My phone vibrates from the floor, but I continue to ignore it. Instead, I put on my workout clothes and head to the hotel gym. For a full hour, I run nonstop on the treadmill, cleansing my body—inside and out—of Wolf. I'm wrecked by the time I make it back to my room and hop in the shower. I allow the warm steam to soak through my pores and fill me until there's no room for anything else.

I finally reach for my phone before hopping into bed and pulling the covers over my chest. There are four messages from Wolf. I cringe before opening them, hoping that reading his texts won't completely sabotage my detox efforts.

9:04 p.m. | Wolf: U ok?

9:35 p.m. | Wolf: Meet me for dinner

10:20 p.m. | Wolf: At club. U should be here. Fuck Crawley. I told that fucker to see a doctor for his stress. He needs medication. Call me.

11:15 p.m. | Wolf: Lyric. U know what! Duck it them.

I'm pretty sure he meant to type *Fuck it then*. Which means two things. He's drunk and done. Whatever he truly means, the last message snaps through my heart as if he's holding the strongest set of pliers. I curse my heart. Not a single ounce of resistance. And I curse Wolf for tying my emotions into knots because that was the one thing I was trying to avoid. It was my entire reason for taking this job.

Another text comes through. I hesitate to open it, but it's screaming at me. I tap the screen and gasp.

12:19 a.m. | Wolf: Im at club, drunk as duck, tits n ass everywhere, but urs r the only ones I wnt in my mouth.

It's hard not to laugh a little. Wolf is confused and drunk. That's all. People don't change overnight, and men who love to play the field certainly don't decide monogamy is for them the moment they meet *the one*. That's the stuff of romance novels. I believe in strength and happiness and loving yourself. Wolf is no knight in shining armor. He's not going to swoop in and fix my fucked-up insecurities. No. If I'm not careful, he will completely ruin me, and I'll be left on the curb mending yet another broken heart.

Convinced that I finally have my shit figured out, I power off my phone and close my eyes, giving my racing heart a few minutes to relax before finally drifting off to sleep.

Chapter Fifteen

Wolf

I hate the chase. Fucking hate it, but there's one thing I hate more: rejection.

What the hell? How did we get here? It's been two weeks since our orgasmathon, and we haven't spoken a word outside of conversations about the tour. Even those are brief and cold—a lot like my showers lately.

Every attempt I've made to get Lyric alone has been skillfully thwarted. It seems like Crawley is on her team, too. Every time I think I've found my chance to talk to her, Crawley swoops in and pulls me in a different direction. I get that he doesn't want the distraction, but it's my life, my band, my tour, my crew… His job description doesn't include being a cockblock.

If I'm honest with myself, though, I haven't made the grandest of attempts to get Lyric alone to talk to her. My ego is still bruised by the words she left me with.

I could let her in. Tell her things. If she only knew what my life was like before she walked into that elevator and how vastly different I want it to be now, she wouldn't be so quick to judge. I never used to think twice about hurting a girl's feelings. All I cared about was making my intentions clear so I could justify my actions.

What Lyric once said about one-night stands turned out to be completely true. I see that now. One person always has expectations coming out of it. Sex is rarely just sex. Even I know that. But I never cared before because I was never the one getting hurt. Sex has never meant anything more than pure fucking pleasure for me, but now it seems I'm getting a taste of my own medicine.

Lyric may be the only woman I'll ever want to claim as my own. She's the only one who makes me crazy at the thought of another guy touching her. Like now, as I stare at her from across my dressing room while she laughs with a guy from security. The same asshole who's made it known to the band and crew the dirty thoughts he's had about Lyric. I want to pummel him. Smash his face into a wall and carry her to our tour bus so I can remind her how my mouth feels on her pretty pussy.

Stryder hands me a shot, and I throw it back without thinking. We're in Columbus, Ohio and have the night off before heading to Louisville, Kentucky first thing in the morning. Which means tonight, we drink.

Lyric's eyes meet mine from across the room. She's mid-laugh, looking gorgeous as ever with my face plastered on her breasts. I think she wears that shit on purpose. Seeing a hot woman in my merch is always a turn on, but Lyric kills the competition. Her innocent eyes search mine briefly before turning back to the security dude. I stand with full intention to head toward her, but she's already making her exit.

Those little glances she's been throwing my way recently tell me this isn't over. Whatever wall she's put up is starting to crumble. Maybe she needed the past two weeks to help her realize this attraction isn't going to fade. She has to know there's been no one else in the time we've spent apart.

Lyric is still mine. Or at least, I'm still hers.

I'll get to the bottom of her resistance, and I'll fix this. It's clear now. There's no other goddamn option.

♪ ♪ ♪

The backstage traffic is heavy tonight. Concert security surrounds me as they clear a controlled walking path. The head of security, a big bald dude who even I wouldn't mess with, leads us toward a waiting area just before the stage. Fans are lined up against the cement block walls, screaming, reaching for me, begging for autographs, trying to snap photos. Lights are popping off, faces become spotty, and I hear the roar.

The waiting crowd is already chanting my name as they eagerly anticipate my howl—it never gets old, even for me—and my adrenaline is pumping triple-speed.

Among the chaos, I see her leaning against the corridor wall like always, watching me as I make my walk to the stage. But this time is different. This time, when I ignore everyone but her and our eyes connect, my heart jolts to life. Even with the screaming crowd ahead of me, she's all I want. And I won't waste another second.

"Over there," I yell to Rex. I point to Lyric and he nods.

Rex the lead, forcing security to follow until I'm right where I want to be—directly in front of Lyric. I lean in and brush my lips across her cheek, stopping at her ear. "Can we talk? After the show?"

Her eyes are as wide as saucers, but she nods.

I smile, loving that I still have this effect on her. With a quick nip at her ear, I continue the walk to the stage to join my band. I don't care who just saw my display of affection. Hopefully everyone. Most won't think anything of it, and the ones who care don't matter. All that matters is ending this silence between us.

One thing is certain as I cross the backstage gap from the hallway to the stage and hear the crowd roar at the opening chords of our intro—this is going to be a great night.

I hang back, and Jimmy, one of our technicians, tosses me my mic. I check for the light, give him a wink, and jump from foot to foot, ready make a run for it when the band hits my cue. The intro morphs into a keyboard solo, and then a drum solo, and then when the guitar riff reaches a scream, I take the four steps in two long strides and run to my mark at center stage.

I plant my feet, arch my back, and howl to the fucking moon. Like always, the crowd responds with an even bigger roar. While they can't hear a thing, I start the first verse of "Joke's On You."

There's something waiting on the other side of fighting
Living like there's nothing, and it's a damn shame
Crying eyes are blinding, temperatures are rising
Back to the beginning, and it's all a lying game

Three songs into the show, I stop to catch my breath. This is the junkie in me right now. Addicted to the sound, to the stage, to the lights blinding everything but where I'm supposed to stand next. I'm not even aware of my movements most of the time. It's like I'm transported to a fucking cloud every time I get on this stage. But there's something extra-special about tonight.

This is my time to talk to the crowd, introduce the band, and kick off "Dangerous Heart." It's been a hit since the San Diego show, but now that the song is officially *ours*, the label has been eating that shit up and promoting it like crazy on social media. We're recording it at the end of the East Coast tour, which will make for a tired-ass week. It was supposed to be our week off. We rarely get breaks on tour, but when recording gets jammed into the schedule, that means less sleep and higher stress for everyone. We don't care, though. We're excited to officially release it and start celebrating our next hit.

"This song, you should all know by now. If you don't, well, pay attention. I stumbled upon these lyrics, and somehow, magically, they became ours. You know those people in life who do things because they love them? Not for the money, not for the fame, but because they have a passion for something? Those people are rare.

"The writer of this song wants to remain anonymous, but I'll have you know, she's fucking incredible. Maybe one day you'll get to meet her, but for now, this song is called 'Dangerous Heart.'"

The crowd responds with the second loudest roar of the night. They all know it already. The way social media took to this song has created a bigger buzz for it than any of our other songs. Even our biggest hits.

I lock eyes with Lyric during the chorus the way I do every single night. Mad at me or not, she's always on the side stage supporting the band—supporting me. After the show, I have every intention of showing her, not telling her, what that means to me.

♪ ♪ ♪

Somehow the backstage crowd has tripled by the time we finish our last song. I'm surrounded by security as they part the way, Rex on my tail.

"Who the fuck invited all these people back here?" I explode when I'm in my dressing room. We couldn't get out the back entrance due to an even bigger crowd outside.

"They're clearing it now. We can leave in ten," Crawley says, pacing. "I'll talk to Lyric."

My eyes narrow darkly at him. There he goes again. His problem with Lyric is goddamn pissing me off. "You and I both know this isn't Lyric's doing. How many passes did the label hand over to the radio stations? I want to know whose fault this is. It makes me look like an asshole when I can't even stop to talk to my fans. I can't even see them beyond security. It's not their fault they were all handed badges. They expect to see us."

"So what do you want to do?" Crawley asks, annoyed.

His constant stress and finger-pointing grates on my last nerve.

"I can set up a meet and greet," a voice calls from across the room. At some point, Lyric entered, and now she stands here, calm as ever. "We can have security keep the line moving so it doesn't take too long, but at least you'll get to see some of your fans."

"Okay," I agree.

Crawley's jaw is ticking. "Fine, but this is on you to set up." He narrows his eyes at her.

She shrugs. "I said I would." Without missing a beat, as always, she pulls out her phone and makes a few phone calls to the promotion teams at the radio stations before radioing the head of security to meet her in my dressing room.

For the hour it takes to set everything up and usher the crowds to a private room, my mind is on Lyric. I'm a jumble when I think about what I want to say to her, wondering how I can possibly convince her I'm not a bad guy. And although I've never been interested in a relationship with anyone before, she makes me want something different. Something more.

When everything is ready, Lyric leads me into the room she had set up. I'm happy to see my band here with me. As much as I want it all to be over, our fans deserve this. Some of them have supported us since we started the band six years ago, and it's because of them that we've catapulted into headlining arenas. The days of being an opening band are far gone. We want to thank the fans whenever we get a chance.

Lyric stops at the table and turns to me, apparently surprised at how close I am. I smile; she looks away, but I catch the flicker of sadness. Whatever the reason for her avoidance, it cracks the surface of my normally ice cold heart. Okay, I've never been heartless, but I've never cared to be understood, either. Until Lyric.

"You're pretty damn amazing, you know that?" I smile warmly. "Thank you for setting this up so quickly. We owe you."

Her eyes are kind as they settle back on mine. When she smiles, my heart does a somersault in my chest. I instinctively reach for her waist but pull my hands back when I hear the commotion at the door. Sighing, I look at the line of fans shuffling in before turning back to Lyric. "Meet me in the hotel lobby when we're done here."

"Okay," she says. "I'm going there now to get everyone checked in, anyway. See you soon."

It seems like the natural thing to do to lean down and brush my lips against hers, but I don't for a million damn reasons. I will be kissing those lips, though. Soon, but not soon enough.

♪ ♪ ♪

By the time we leave the venue, my body is wrecked from exhaustion and I'm fighting to keep my eyes open. The guys went straight to the bar after the meet and greet, so I'm riding back to the hotel with Rex. When I see Lyric waiting for me in the lobby, just as I asked, I want to melt. She changed into black capri leggings and a Wolf hoodie. Fucking gorgeous.

She glances up from her phone and watches me approach, concern etched in her features. "You okay?"

I don't respond right away. Instead, I wrap my arms around her and bury my face in her neck. When I take in her scent, sparks light up in my chest at the sheer pleasure of it. Up until this moment, I've respected the distance Lyric was keeping between us, but I can't stay away from her anymore.

It's killing me. This—holding her, breathing her in—it's everything I never knew I wanted until I met her.

To my surprise, she returns my embrace and tightens her hold around my waist, filling my chest with warmth. "What's wrong?"

"Everything. I just need this. And I'm wrecked after today."

"Should we go somewhere?" Her voice is muffled in my shoulder, but I hear her.

I nod. "I can barely keep my eyes open. Let's go to my room." She freezes in my hold, so I pull myself away to look her in her eyes. "Just to talk, Lyric. And I want to hold you." I brush my finger across her cheek, loving the way she looks back at me now—like she's conflicted, but there's no way she's going to deny my needs.

"Your room or mine?"

I know there's a ridiculous smile on my face when she blushes and leads me to the elevator. We get in, and I wrap my arms around her from behind, never wanting to let go. After tonight, I hope I never do.

Once we're safely inside her hotel room, I head for the bathroom first. I've been going nonstop for hours, and my bladder is about to explode. I'd kill for a shower, but I'm not sacrificing any of the precious time I have with Lyric.

She's sitting on the bed when I enter the room, her feet dangling off the edge and her head down as if she's in deep thought. I sit beside her, making no move to touch her, although it's all I want to do. I'm stunned when she speaks first. "That was nice what you said about me tonight. On stage."

I look at her. "I meant it."

Her next breath is a deep one, drawing my eyes to the rise and fall of her chest, but I catch myself and immediately lift them to her face. Tonight isn't about sex. Lyric deserves more.

"Look, these two weeks have been hell. I'm not sure if your avoiding me has more to do with Crawley or my reputation, but you should know I'm not going to let Crawley be the reason you can't even look at me anymore. I'll deal with him."

Her lids flutter closed for a second before her eyes land on mine again. I suck in a breath to stop myself from throwing her back on the bed and claiming her mouth.

"It's not Crawley," she sighs. "What he said to me didn't help the situation—"

I heat up immediately. "What did Crawley say?"

She shakes her head. "Some shit about my reputation and your todger." She surprises me by giggling. It's so fucking adorable, I melt. "He may have been out of line, but he was right. I'm here to do a job, and it's obvious I can't do my job if we're messing around."

I groan and turn to face her. "That was the hotel's mess-up, Lyric. Otherwise, they wouldn't have scrambled to find accommodations for everyone and then paid for it. They fucked up. Not you. Stop beating yourself up. And stop using that as an excuse as to why you ignored every single one of my messages that night and every attempt I've made to talk to you since. I wanted to respect your space. Part of me started to think maybe the distance was a good thing."

Shaking my head, I bite back a frustrated growl. "What I feel for you isn't normal—for me. I can't promise you the world like you deserve. All I know is I've been miserable since that day. It doesn't help that you have zero reason to think more of me."

"Wolf, it's not that I don't think more of you. You've surprised me. I didn't expect to—" she shakes her head. "I would have slept with you, and then what? You go back to your lineup of women, and I go back to being just your road manager?"

My chest puffs. "Have you seen me so much as talk to any of those women who've come around?"

She doesn't hesitate before shaking her head, which tells me she's already thought of this. Good. "I guess not."

"Why do you think that is?"

She shrugs, avoiding my eyes.

I groan. "Lyric, you're the only one I see. When I'm singing to a sea of faces, *yours* is the one I look for. The moment we step back on the bus, *you're* the one I want to spend my time with."

Her mouth drops open, and there are tears in her eyes. "But what does that mean, Wolf? You've suddenly changed? And I'm not just talking about the rumors. I'm referring to conversations you and I have had. You told me I wasn't your type, and then you made it clear that you don't date. It didn't matter to me because I didn't come on this tour looking for anything. I was running away from one thing that was bad for my heart, and I ran smack into another."

My insides squeeze as a tear slips from her eye. I wipe it away the moment it hits her cheek. "It's a *good* thing you're not my type. We both know what I was doing before I met you. And I can't promise I'm a changed man. I don't know what this is between us, okay? What I can tell you is that I'll be completely honest with you while we figure this shit out. Because I want to figure it out. Don't you?"

She nods and takes a ragged breath. I let out a sigh and lean my forehead on hers. "Thank fuck." She laughs. "Now that we've settled that," I say as I pull her to her feet and tilt her chin up until our eyes meet. "I'm not leaving your side tonight, so either I stay here with you or you come to my room. No sex," I say, letting the promise linger in the air. "Just let me hold you."

I hear her intake of breath, and it fills me with warmth.

"You can stay." It's barely a whisper.

"Good," I growl with a puff of my chest. Damn, this feels good. Just being here.

I don't want to leave her for even a second, but if I'm going to sleep with Lyric, my balls should be fresh. Even if she won't be touching them. I cry a little inside. "Before I climb in next to your sexy ass, I need a shower. Don't disappear on me, okay?"

She smiles shyly and my insides go crazy.

"Go," she says with a little shove.

I'm not sure if jacking off in the shower will help or hurt me tonight, but I do it anyway, praying the release holds me over until I can take care of myself again in the morning. I meant what I said to Lyric about no sex. Tonight wasn't a ploy to get into bed with her.

I groan as I empty myself, the dirty thoughts of Lyric suddenly turning into something surprising. Something sweeter. Kissing Lyric's soft lips.

Just kissing her.

I'm out of the shower in record time and throw a towel around my waist. Rex must have dropped off my overnight bag with Lyric because it's sitting on the bathroom counter. Which means she was in here while I was jacking off to thoughts of her. I smirk, wondering if she heard anything.

After digging around in my bag, I find everything I need. I apply deodorant, run a comb through my hair, and throw on a pair of boxer briefs and shorts. It's suffocating but safe. After some hesitation, I decide to put on a shirt, too.

She's already under the covers when I flip off the bathroom light and make my way to her. I slip under the comforter and immediately pull her to me so my fully clothed, limp dick is nestled between her ass cheeks and my nose is in her hair. She smells like heaven, and the thin fabric of her tank top is soft against my skin.

I brush a strand of her long hair off her neck and dip down to taste the flesh of her shoulder with a light bite, lick, and kiss. Her moan is soft and encouraging, so I do it again. My dick isn't limp anymore, and I realize tonight might hurt—a lot. We rest there for a minute before either of us speaks.

"You never talk about your dad," she says quietly. My heart beats a little faster, realizing that I want to tell her everything. How is that possible? We've only known each other a few weeks and I'm ready to divulge my entire life history to her. Maybe because I know we've led similar lives. God knows she didn't have it easy with Mitch Cassidy and Destiny Lane as her parents.

"There's not much to talk about, Lyric. He was never around. His music came first, which I get … now … but still, he had a family, you know? Never once were we the priority. I got used to hating him. Now, I just don't think about him."

She sighs softly. "Do you hear about him now? Do you know where he is?"

I chuckle lightly. "No, and I don't care. I can't fix him. There was a time I thought I could, but that was me being young and optimistic. I believed anything was possible. He just ... didn't care. And I'll never understand it. I can't imagine forgiving him, and I've learned to live with that."

"I know how you feel," she says, her tone saddened most likely by her own memories.

From the moment we met, there was a connection. I didn't get it at first. I just thought Lyric was a hot chick with something to prove who was joining the tour. I expected her to be a pain in my ass, and part of me wanted to egg her on. But something changed the moment I knew she wrote the lyrics of that song. It was like she came into my life at the exact moment I needed her to. I don't know what any of it means other than the fact that I'm ready to let this play out instead of slamming the door on it. Whatever *it* is.

With a feather-light touch, I drag my fingers down Lyric's arm until I reach her hand. Twining our fingers together, I squeeze, and then press against her again. Her breathing comes in heavy pants that speak directly to my aching balls. She doesn't have to tell me she wants me. The tiny noises coming from her throat and the way her ass pushes into me tells me everything I need to know.

"We're not having sex tonight," I repeat as she grinds her backside against me, causing me to grit my teeth.

I unravel our fingers and slide my hand back up her body until I reach the bottom of her tank top and slip it beneath the fabric. I'm aching to touching her silky soft skin.

Moving my hand up further, I grip her bare waist and press into her again. "Turn around."

When she's facing me, she bats her eyes, then places a hand at the bottom of my shirt and tugs upwards.

I lift my hands over my head and allow her to remove it, leaving my chest bare for her searching fingers. She's focused on every detail, leaving chills behind every touch. I'm so interested in what she's doing to me that I forget about touching her. My entire body is vibrating. And then her hands reach the waistband of my shorts.

"Off," she commands.

My body goes tense, and I stare at her with warning. My dick jerks with excitement as if he knows she's coming after him. "Lyric."

"No sex tonight, but I want to feel you."

Fuck.

I tug the shorts off quickly and kick them to the end of the bed. "Better?" I ask huskily.

She smiles and shifts so her legs are intertwined with mine, and then she presses a sweet kiss below one pec, creating a buzz throughout my body. Just the feel of her lips on my skin is too much.

She continues to place kisses across my chest, working her way up to my neck. When she reaches her destination, I groan and place my hand on the back of her neck, massaging it slowly as my raging erection continues to dig into her.

Every movement causes my balls to ache a little more, but I can't get over the fact that her lips have touched most of my body except my lips. I need her mouth. Now.

In a swift move, my mouth catches hers before she can drag her lips down again. It's the softest of kisses, and I enjoy every damn second of it. Her lips are plush, like my favorite kind of pillow. Conforming to my every direction. Sinking and lifting. Warming at every contact. Like everything else about Lyric, her lips are perfect.

I've never had to restrain myself before. When I want a woman, I take her. Holding back for Lyric is making me crazy in so many ways.

Our breaths collide before I press down on her lips again, showing her just how much my mouth needs hers. My tongue finds its entrance and dips into the warmth, earning a moan from her. Lyric's grip tightens on my waist before she slides her hands over my ass and squeezes.

I growl and push my length against her stomach, making her gasp. "No sex," I say again because she's either forgotten or trying to kill me with all the touching.

She giggles, slipping her index finger under the fabric of my underwear and sliding it around until she's touching the nest of hair at my groin. My heart pounds at the thought of her hands on me again. It's been too long. "Goddamn, Lyric," I moan as her hand travels lower. I want her so bad. She can't keep touching me like this.

And then she wraps her small hands around my engorged length and squeezes.

I gasp, my vision blurs, my heart beats double-time, and then it's game over.

My teeth tug at her bottom lip before I remove her tank top. I hate that she has to remove her hands from me, but we'll get back to that. Right now, I need her tits in my mouth.

I sigh before taking a mouthful and swirling my tongue over her skin until she lets out a scream. My free hand keeps busy, too, working its way down to her underwear and slipping a finger over the fabric that covers her clit. I circle my finger and I suck at her nipples until she gives me more of those tiny noises I love to hear.

I almost explode the moment she pushes against my chest, climbs on top of me, and slips my briefs down enough to release my erection. "Wait here," she pants as she rolls over and removes her underwear.

Just as quickly, she's on top of me again and plants her mouth on mine with a groan. I'm speechless when she removes her mouth for a moment and reaches down to plunge her fingers into herself before spreading the wetness around her pussy. When she's satisfied, she pushes my throbbing dick against my stomach and moves against it as her hand strokes the underside.

I'm going to lose it. She's not pushing me into her. Instead, she's using the length of my dick as her riding stick, fucking me with those pretty lips while jacking me off. This is new. And while she's getting us both off, I get to watch her face. Her eyes are closed, but her mouth is slightly parted and releasing little pants of air with each movement. Her gorgeous breasts bounce above me, and her tiny waist moves with controlled, skillful movements that roll her sexy hips against me. *Damn.*

I watch as her need for a release overcomes her. It's sexy as hell, and it looks like she's about to come any second. I grip her waist, slowing her movements slightly as she starts convulsing above me. With a quick move, I'm replacing her weakened hold on my cock and stroking myself, releasing my buildup while watching her clit throb and her body shudder above me.

"Holy shit," she mewls.

Holy shit is right.

I pull her down so her body is flush against mine and take her mouth, kissing the hell out of her. When I pull away, I chuckle. "That was the best non-sex I've ever had."

She laughs and rolls off me, still trying to catch her breath. "Yeah," is all she manages to say before we pass out in each other's arms.

Chapter Sixteen

Lyric

No regrets. Not a single one. As I awaken from an incredible dream having everything to do with Wolf and his magical mouth, I slowly become aware of the wet sensations between my thighs. Tongue swirling, mouth sucking. I gasp, already close to the edge, and I'm not even fully awake yet.

After I come out of my orgasmic oasis, Wolf lifts up so his body is covering mine and kisses me hard, letting me taste myself.

"Good morning," he greets huskily. Wolf's voice is hot as sin in the morning.

His shaft is stiff between my legs, rocking into me as if begging for permission to enter. But he holds back, keeping his promise.

"Good morning to you." I smile as he buries his mouth in my neck and groans. "You're extra awake this morning," I tease.

"I can't believe I slept with you naked beside me. I've never done that before you. Ever."

"Slept with someone without having sex?"

He nods into my hair. "Uh-huh. And this is the second time with you." Something about the sweetness in his voice

Oh, God. For a moment I'm frozen, just watching him, trying to make sense of what I'm seeing. The tightness in my chest and pressure in my throat build as I witness his pain, telling me that my feelings for this man go beyond anything rational. These feelings weren't planned. They weren't even wanted or welcomed. But they're here in this room and there's no denying it anymore.

I push the door all the way open, approach him, and place my arms around his waist with my face pressed against his back. He continues to let go, silent sobs of pain pulling from deep within him.

I want to be strong for him. Hold him for as long as he wants or needs. And then a tear falls onto my arm, and it completely rips me apart. Now I'm crying with him. My hands move up his chest until one is directly above his heart, as if I can hold it in place for him. I don't know why or how it happened, but Wolf's pain is now my own.

♪ ♪ ♪

No words were spoken in the bathroom. After crying together for what felt like forever, both our phones began to ring like crazy. I finally took the call to hear Crawley scream at me on the other end. I lied. I told him I didn't know where Wolf was, but I was on my way to his room and we'd be to the bus shortly. Once on the bus, Wolf went straight to his room, and I could tell by his swift departure that he wanted to be alone.

I ignore Crawley's heated stare the entire first hour back on the bus before giving up and taking refuge in my bunk. We have an eight-hour drive ahead of us to Wisconsin, which means one long pit stop to give Rory a break at the wheel. Tonight, we sleep on the bus.

I nap for a few hours, and when I awake, I grab my laptop to do some work. There are over three hundred messages in my inbox, most of which are confirmations for upcoming accommodations, but it's too much for my brain right now. I can't get Wolf—and the confusion I feel after witnessing his tears—off my mind.

I'm not confused by my feelings for him; those were solidified last night when he told me I'm the only one he sees, and then again this morning when he said it was like I was made for him. Those words were heavy for both of us. No, I'm confused by his reaction. What did I say that made him break down like that?

Knowing getting through my emails is impossible, I close my laptop and reach for my songbook at the corner of my bed. I open it to find my latest unfinished piece and start writing.

Chapter Seventeen

Wolf

The question isn't whether I want Lyric by my side. And there isn't a speck of doubt that she would be here if I asked. The problem is the self-consuming hole of darkness I tumbled into the moment Lyric said she wanted to meet my mother. It sent me down a mental path I've avoided for so long. Four years, to be exact. Never in my wildest dreams did I expect to unleash that on her, but after her comment, there was no stopping the volcano of emotions that rose in my chest. And then she had to watch me physically fall apart in the bathroom. I cried like a fucking baby, and she saw every single teardrop.

Then she held me.

Besides my sister, I've loved one woman and one woman only. My mother. When she was dying, we spoke of my future. I made promises to her, some I've been able to fulfill, others I haven't. Have I respected every woman I've encountered? Not in a way that my mother would be proud of. Have I worked hard and stayed true to my dreams? Without a doubt. Have I met someone who makes every other flower wilt in comparison? Hell yes. Do I have any intention of pursuing the connection? That's where shit gets complicated.

I didn't think my heart was capable of beating this way for anyone, not even someone as beautiful and smart and sexy as Lyric. My mother's death suffocated a part of me until it grew cold and died. Letting someone in means letting them see all of me—the damage, the hurt, the pain, the bitterness I have toward life beyond the music. I've always thought there's no way in hell I would open myself up to anyone if it meant being vulnerable like that. I'd always been the strong one. As my mother was fading away, I squeezed her hand, letting her know I would be okay when she was gone and could no longer look after me. But even as I made those promises, I knew they were all sugarcoated lies to mask my pain and make her death as peaceful as possible.

The lies hurt like hell. They still do.

While I promised my mother one thing, I silently promised myself something different. Falling in love was never the plan.

When Lyric said she wanted to meet my mother, it all came crashing down. My first thought was that my mother would have adored her. She'd have given me that knowing smile, like when I'd made a decision she was proud of but she expected no differently because she believed in me. And then the realization hit like a boulder slowly rolling over me and crushing my chest; I let my attraction for someone completely obliterate my vow—a vow I made for a damn good reason. Because loving someone hurts like hell when it ends.

So how do I explain this story to the one person who needs to hear it in order to understand me? How do I trust someone enough to have that kind of control over the one thing that's ever made me vulnerable?

There's a tap at my door, but I ignore it. Then comes another before it opens, and Lyric lets herself in. I watch her beautiful body as she quietly closes the door and leans against it, a mixture of pain and sorrow painted on her face.

I caused this. I led her on. For a second, I believed I could do this—be with her in a way that was more than sex and an ego boost.

"We don't have to talk about it," she says. It's then that I see her songbook clutched to her chest. "I wrote something. Will you read it?"

I can almost feel her heart pounding. The way she's letting her vulnerability bleed into my room, she's asking me to trust her without asking anything at all. If I had to name the thing I love most about Lyric, it just might be the emotions and stories she's able to express on paper. It's my ultimate weakness, which is why, despite my intention to let her go, I nod.

Her steps are slow. Her eyes are everywhere but on mine. And then she sits on my bed, handing me her open book. I take it and then I pull her down so that she's lying by my side. Her free arm wraps around my waist and her cheek rests on my chest. I'm sure she can feel my heart racing at our nearness.

The title, "Taste," catches my attention. My eyes drag across the words slowly, allowing every single one to sink in until I can feel the emotions compounding in my chest.

Taste

You've stolen a piece without asking for consent
Not in my plans to fall to my knees

It's simply meant to be
Tell me, how does it feel?

Tasting flesh so hungrily
That smile on your face aches in me
My lust for you is shaking
I'm yours for the taking
Tell me, how does it feel?

Give me another taste
You know you're craving me
Let me have another taste
As I lose myself to you
Give me another taste
While you steal more of me

Not sure how this will end
Stealing pieces of me till you win
Silent war between heart and mind
Heart wins out every time

I wish it were that easy.

      Lyric takes the book from my hands and sets it on the floor before facing me again. When she plants her soft lips on mine, her lyrics run through my mind again, blinding me. My response to her words is revealed in my response to her kiss. I take over, gently moving her so that she's beneath me. My tongue dives in to explore her mouth and all its warmth. I keep my movements achingly slow as I let my passion pour into her.

I peel the layers of clothes from our bodies and get to work placing my mouth on all her most sensitive places. Then I beg her to look at me. I'm positioned above her, her legs spread wide to accommodate me. The condom is hugging me, unwelcome but necessary, and I'm ready to finally enter her. But I can't be inside her unless I'm staring into her eyes. I can see every emotion in them as if their depths could carry me straight to her heart. When our eyes lock, I let out a sigh and remove my finger from her core, exchanging it for the tip of my shaft.

"You're beautiful, Lyric."

I already know that with Lyric, it will be more than just a release. Once I have her, I'm not sure I'll be able to toss her aside like I do the others. I may want seconds, and thirds, and who the fuck knows how long that will last.

Her breath catches when I push into her. So I go slow, letting her get used to me first, and then I sink deeply, as far as our bodies will allow. For a moment, I just kiss her while her tightness hugs me enough to make me forget to breathe. Her high-pitched sigh causes me to thicken inside her, and then I'm moving, pushing into her with slow strokes, our eyes never breaking their hold.

I'm completely lost in her—in us—the pleasure becoming too much. But she's there with me, our heated breaths colliding.

When her fingertips dig into my shoulders and her movements take over, controlling every thrust, I feel my own build intensify.

"Lyric," I warn.

She releases a stuttered breath. "Wolf," she whimpers.

The tone behind my name is my undoing, and I take control back, rocking my hips into hers with more demanding thrusts. I bury my face in her neck, tasting the sweat rolling down her skin before biting into it as she shakes with her release. Her tightness clenches around me over and over as I pound into her again and again.

With a grunt, my own orgasm erupts into the condom, into her. When the final ounce of me is released, I'm still shaking. My tense muscles relax and I collapse, holding my weight but never wanting to leave her warmth. Not that she'd let me. Lyric's arms and legs are wrapped tightly around me, her breaths fighting against my chest.

"Holy shit," I say with a rush of air. "What the fuck was that?" I look down at her.

She bites her lip and releases it quickly before smiling. "I think you liked my song."

I feel my entire body soften at her words. It forces me to remember what brought us to this point—to the aftermath of the best sex in the world.

"I loved it," I reply honestly.

When I return to the bed after disposing of the condom, Lyric is still lying naked, staring out the window with a thoughtful expression. She said we didn't need to talk about it, but how can I hold back after that? After she poured her heart out to me in the form of lyrics and after we shared the most intense sex I've ever had?

I climb onto the bed, wrap my arms around her, and kiss her cheek. Sliding my hand down, I circle the dark peaks of her breasts with my finger, all the while still looking into her eyes. "You're beautiful," I breathe. "If I say it too much, I'm sorry, but you're the most beautiful fucking thing."

When Lyric smiles, it's always genuine and always starts from her eyes. "You're not so bad yourself."

For this next part, I need to look away. I rest my cheek on her chest and tell her the story of my mother.

"My mom was diagnosed with cervical cancer when I was sixteen. I was still in high school, and I didn't cope well. I was terrified I would lose my mom, fighting with anyone who ever gave me shit about anything. Suspensions were frequent, and music was my only outlet. Even as sick as she was, she swore she'd beat the living shit out of me if I didn't smart up." I chuckle over the tightness in my chest.

"I listened to her, graduated from high school, and then spent every free moment trying to take care of her. Still made time for my music because it was the only thing that kept me from feeling like drowning. My sister helped as much as she could between work and school, and she'd take over when I'd have gigs. But my mom kept getting worse.

"Chemo made her miserable, and the cancer was spreading. So I stayed at home and took some online classes, but I knew I didn't want to go the college route. I was cooking, cleaning, taking her to doctor appointments. To the hospital when she'd..." My voice catches.

Lyric turns to wrap an arm around me. She rests her cheek on my chest and my breathing slows again, enough to continue.

"My father was on the road a lot, and when she started to get worse, he just disappeared. I'd follow his tour online and would know when his time off was, but he never came home. Never even called. I'd see pictures of him all over the internet with half-naked groupies slung over each arm. I died inside thinking my mother might see the same things. My mom was a fucking angel. She never wanted me to feel bad, so she didn't say a word. But I know she was so hurt, Lyric."

I take a ragged breath, trying desperately not to get worked up.

"And then she was at the hospital again. Doctors said she was close to death. My dad still never showed up.

"My mom would always talk to me about the things she wished for me. She'd beg me to make her promises about how I would treat women . . . that I would choose *the one* carefully." My eyes flicker to Lyric, who's tracing light circles on my skin. "And that when I found her, she would be it for me. She never said it, but I know she didn't want me to become my father.

"I made those promises to her. Every single one. But I've done a shit job of seeing them through. When she passed, I went straight to my music and buried myself in it. Let it consume me. That's been my last four years. Sex, booze, and rock 'n' roll. It was therapeutic in a sense. It helped me repress the excruciating pain of my mom leaving this world, but I know she's probably rolling over in her grave with disappointment."

"You make it sound like you've been living in sin for four years," Lyric says gently. "You were mourning your mother's death. It's natural to not deal with death right away. I can't imagine losing someone so close to me, but I don't think it's something you ever fully heal from. You're going to make mistakes, Wolf. It's never too late to make better decisions."

My sweet Lyric. So optimistic. I lean in to kiss her again. If anything can illuminate the darkness, it's the feelings I have for this woman right here.

"I wrote something, too," I confess.

Her eyes widen. "Can I read it?"

I take a deep breath and reach for my notebook under the bed. I flip it open in front of her until it lands on the last page I wrote in. My eyes are on her as my heart beats wildly in my chest, watching her reactions to my lyrics about my new favorite subject: her.

Free Me

My soul is dark, so dark and deadly
Twisted, angry, misunderstood
Don't get too close, you're not ready
It's all-consuming and you're too good

It's deep, this well I've fallen into
I'm caught with dirt beneath my nails
I dug the hole myself
But I'm trying to climb, until I realize
You're not mine

Free me, free me
Give me a reason to climb
I want to make you mine
You're the only light
Free me, free me

Darkness is cold, so cold and lonely
Blanketing me with nothing
Except hollowed hopes and shattered dreams
Your light is all the reason to sing

There are tears in her eyes when she's done reading, and she shifts so she's above me, straddling my body and looking down at me with a wicked gleam. My dick grows at the sight—every curve illuminated with the light filtering in through the cracks in the blinds. Specks of dust float beneath the light, but they might as well be flecks of glitter. She's a fucking angel. My angel.

I reach for her waist, but she shakes her head slowly. She places my hands near my head, her breasts dangling near my mouth. I taste one in passing, causing her to smile. I lift my head and place my folded hands behind it. "You're up to something," I say with a smile.

She doesn't respond. Instead, she runs the tips of her fingers down my arms, chest, and stomach. Her eyes flicker to mine before she leans down and presses her lips directly above my heart. I swear when she does that it blooms in my chest. All my heart needed were the right ingredients to bring me back to life. Lyric is my light, my water, my soil, my sun. My eyes drink her in, appreciating her. I sigh. She's my everything.

She reaches over to my drawer, grabs another condom, and rolls it over my cock. All the while, I'm consumed by the confidence and blinding beauty in her movements.

When she lifts onto her knees and rubs herself, I move my arms to help her out but put them back when she shoots me a look that's playfully fierce. "Hands behind your head."

I grin, happy to obey. She dips a finger into herself, causing a groan to escape from deep in my chest. I fucking love when she does that.

She positions her body above me and sinks down, her head falling back, sighing at the fullness. I'll need all my concentration if I'm going to last with this sight in front of me.

She begins to move, her hands pressing against my chest, her back arching at just the right moments, her breasts full and begging to be touched.

When the first bead of sweat rolls down her forehead, I don't know what comes over me, but I have the distinct desire to tell her I love her. But since it's quite possibly motivated by her bouncing tits and come-face, I hold back. I do, however, begin to feel a voracious, mind-shattering force taking over my entire body before it numbs me helpless. It's followed by a rush of adrenaline as we come together, moaning and silently screaming each other's names.

Chapter Eighteen

Lyric

Aragon Ballroom in Chicago is my favorite venue. My dad moved us to the area when I was twelve. It was the first place besides the tour bus that I remember calling home. He purchased a condo in downtown Chicago on North Burling Street. A luxury building that resembled a palace, with gold-wrapped iron banisters and a courtyard garden that looked like it belonged in a Disney movie.

Our condo was spacious, but my father managed to make it feel homey. And while he still did light traveling to record songs and attend events, he was spending time with me. He'd perform at local venues regularly to keep busy, and when he wasn't performing, we'd attend other shows at the Aragon. I quickly became well-acquainted with the venue, regulars, and staff. It was my home. They were my family.

It's late morning when we arrive at the venue. The familiar brick exterior brings back nostalgia for a time of pure happiness. When my father took a break from life on the road and made me a priority. At least, he tried. For three years, to be exact. That's more than I can ever give my mom credit for.

We line up and eagerly make our way to the front of the tour bus. Everyone's hungry and stiff from the overnight ride. Wolf and I are last in line, staying a safe distance from each other so no one suspects that we spent the entire night having quiet, intense sex.

Rory holds the door for us while Crawley and Rex have a heated discussion on the curb. Wolf surprises me by holding me back, then signals to Rory to close the door to give us some privacy. I laugh, trying to figure out what's going on.

Once we're alone, Wolf turns me around and pulls me into his arms, slamming his mouth against mine. I instinctively mold myself to his body, turned on by the urgency behind his kiss. It feels like he's about to swallow me, the way his tongue glides ravenously over mine. I groan into his mouth and tighten my grip on his sides before slipping my hands beneath his shirt and up his bare stomach. God, I could run my tongue along these ridges all day long.

For the past week, we've managed to keep our hands off each other—except for in private. The moment the guys go to sleep every night, I slip out of my bunk and into Wolf's waiting arms. And during our hotel stays, we only check into one room. We've also limited our club nights, preferring to spend the time alone together.

Restraint becomes more difficult every single day because it physically hurts to be near Wolf without being able to pounce on him. Moments alone feel stolen, like we're on borrowed time ... like now.

He scoops me up and sits down on the couch, placing my legs on either side of him. I press down, wanting desperately to release the erection from his pants. The friction of his jeans grating against me is eliciting heavy pants, and I need more.

We should be naked. Now. I want nothing more than to ride him just like this so he can peer up at me while I take control. I love the way Wolf looks at me when I'm on top. Like I'm both angel and devil. Pleasing him and torturing him with every movement.

He takes his mouth from mine and brings slow suction to my neck in a way that always escalates my heart rate until I feel like I'm going to lose my mind.

"I want you. Now," I moan.

He growls before biting down and pressing my hips onto his lap, helping me feel more of him.

"Wolf," I whine. Why is he teasing me?

His mouth comes off my neck, and he examines my dress for a second before slipping a finger under the material and landing on my clit. He rubs it through my underwear, caressing my heat with gentle strokes like he's dreaming of getting inside me.

He watches my face morph from need to pleasure and smiles wickedly. "Not now, baby. I have plans for you later." He removes his finger and smooths out my dress.

When he lifts me from his lap and places me on my feet, I'm all glares. "Seriously?" My hands land on my hips. "You wanted to be alone with me to turn me down?"

"Babe," he says with a laugh, standing and pulling me toward him again. I don't want to shiver in his hold, but my resolve is shot after his rejection. "Work, remember?"

He's throwing my words back at me. Payback for rejecting him in his dressing room last night before he was about to go on stage. I pout. But in my defense, I didn't want to be responsible for thousands of enraged fans waiting for his howl.

He's not supposed to be the one reminding me that we need to focus on the job. He's supposed to throw me over his shoulder and drag me to his room, caveman style, and make me forget everything except how perfectly his body fits with mine.

My anger dissipates when I glance into his soft, caramel eyes. I want to melt into them, even if that means becoming a sticky, gooey, messy blob of sugar. I can do that. Only for Wolf.

"What plans do you have, exactly?" I ask.

"Well..." He sweeps a lock of hair over my shoulder and strokes my cheek with his thumb. "I recall promising you a date. So you're mine tonight before I go on stage."

I sigh. "You know I have to work before you go on stage."

He smiles. "I've taken care of that. You're off-duty tonight. All you need to worry about is wearing some fuck-hot heels. I don't even care what you wear above them because as soon as we're done with dinner, all you'll be wearing are those shoes when I pound you senseless against the wall."

Holy shit.

"Sounds like a romantic *date*," I say with a wiggle of my shoulders.

His mouth twists up in a grin. "Baby, after you see what I have planned for tonight, you'll have a new definition of romance."

I laugh at his promise. "Can't wait."

We step off the bus together to find Crawley waiting with his arms crossed. Rex is behind him, looking annoyed, but I get the distinct feeling it's aimed at Crawley, not us.

"What were you two doing?" Crawley asks, his tone accusing.

"Business, Crawley," Wolf answers casually.

With a shake of his head, it seems as if Crawley's about to let whatever's bunched up his panties go. Wishful thinking on my part, I guess. "If you two think you're fooling anyone on this bus, I'd like to be the first to tell you you're not."

"Okay, great. Thanks, Crawley." Wolf pulls me toward the back entrance of the venue before Crawley can say another word. He's radiating intensity, and I can tell he's pissed about the confrontation.

"Just ignore him," I say with a squeeze of my hand. "He's not used to seeing you with anyone. Give him time to get over it. He will." As I'm saying this, I'm not so sure.

Wolf narrows his eyes. I think he's about to argue with me, but then his lips curl up in a smile and he leans in to kiss me. Crawley walks through the door after us, and I can sense him debating whether he should say something. When he finally breezes by, uttering curse words under his breath, our laughter breaks up our lip-lock.

"I'm glad Crawley said something," Wolf murmurs into my neck. "Now there's nothing stopping me from making you scream the next time I fuck you on that bus."

Shit. Every time Wolf and I have had sex, it's been gentle and full of exploration. Always intense. It's been perfect. But now, I can't help but imagine his rough hands on me as he presses me against the wall and drills me into tomorrow.

He squeezes my ass and runs toward the stage with a huge grin spread across his face.

♪ ♪ ♪

I call for a car and head to the hotel before the band is finished with their soundcheck to get everyone checked in by the time they arrive. I stand there with the keys, handing them out as always.

Wolf approaches last, winking at me.

"One keycard for the rock god, Wolf," I say and reach my hand out with a bat of my eyelashes.

He pulls me to him with a grin, causing his bandmates, crew, and even some strangers, to turn and stare. A rush of excitement licks through me at our public display. Wolf meant it when he said he was glad everyone knew about us. He's done hiding it. "Thanks, babe. I'll come get you at your room at five, okay? I have some things I need to do before we leave."

I try to ignore my disappointment. Wolf and I have been sharing a hotel room since last week. I wasn't planning to get my own. "Okay. I'll text you my room number."

He kisses me on the cheek and takes off for the elevator after Derrick and Hedge. *That was strange.* Wolf never misses an opportunity to trap me in an elevator. I shrug it off, check into my room, and jump into the shower. Maybe having my own room is a good thing. I can take as long as I want in here without being mauled by Wolf's sexy hands.

Three new text messages are waiting for me when I'm done in the shower. Still wrapped in my towel, I lay on my bed to go through them.

12:32 p.m. | **Asshole:** Hey, baby girl. Just writing to say I miss you.

I laugh at the name I programmed for Tony in my phone. *Is he for real?*

12:46 p.m. | **Asshole:** I fucked up. I'm going to make this right.

>*Oh, hell no, you won't.*
>
>I block his number. The next message is from Wolf, asking for my room number. I quickly reply and start mentally preparing for our date.
>
>I'm wearing a short, floral skirt and a faded jean jacket when the knock sounds at my door at five on the dot. Even after spending every day of the past week with Wolf, the little flutters still come alive in my chest at the thought of him. I open the door, and—*holy shit.*
>
>He's standing there dressed in dark, ripped jeans, a thin, white V-neck shirt, and a navy blazer with the sleeves rolled up. Wolf is out-of-this-world good-looking, and even more so when he smiles at me like he is now.
>
>"Beautiful," he says, eyeing me.
>
>I make a point to twirl and lift a foot when I'm done, pointing to a heel. Just as promised. "You like?"
>
>His eyes blaze as he hungrily takes me in. I know he's imagining what he wants to do to me later, and it makes me grow hot under his spell. "I approve," he says in all seriousness.
>
>I take a step forward and drag my hand down his chest, never pulling my eyes from his. "You look good

enough to eat." Then I slip my arms around his waist underneath his blazer. "I know this is our first date and all, but I'm really hoping you aren't going to make me sleep alone tonight."

His amused smile illuminates his entire face, and he leans his forehead against mine. "Oh no, babe. I have plans for you." Then he brings his mouth against my ear. "All night."

Shivers run through me like wildfire, but he doesn't give me time to recover as he takes me by the hand and guides me toward the elevator. The car is waiting for us at the curb. Wolf holds the door open for me, and I slide in to find a single rose waiting on the seat along with a card. I open it as Wolf steps around to the other side of the car.

Lyric,
To some, words are cheap. For us, words are everything. Here are mine:

From the moment I met you, there was something about you that would not leave me. What you sparked when your hands fell onto my chest in that elevator only ignited when our eyes met, and it's a flame that still burns between us. Like one of those damn trick candles. I hope this one burns forever.

Here's to our first date and to every moment after.

Wolf

This is why I love lyricists and why I'm crazy about Wolf in particular. Well, it's one of the many reasons. His words seep into my cracked exterior and soak my heart, turning it to mush.

I'm done reading by the time Wolf sinks into the seat beside me, and I have to restrain myself from straddling him. Instead, I reach out to hold his hand. Once our fingers are tangled together, he squeezes my hand, and I feel it again. The intense flame that burns between us. It may not have been in my plans to fall for Wolf, but it's clear now that I never had a choice. This thing happening between us, whatever it is, is meant to be.

Chapter Nineteen

Wolf

She's breathtaking. I'm not sure how I'm resisting her because everything about Lyric screams "take me now," from her shiny, purple heels to the way she's looking at me like she wants to jump me. The way that flowery skirt rides up her glossy thigh. *Fuck me.* And the way her little hand slides into mine after reading the letter—that small gesture she offers me is enough to boost my confidence. Truth be told, I need the confidence boost.

Lyric will never know it, but I'm fucking nervous. I spent the whole day setting up for our night, wondering if I was completely losing my mind. Not only has she hooked my heart, but she's reeling me in without any effort at all. It's been over two weeks since I promised Lyric a date, and she hasn't said a word about it. I'm not even sure she remembers, but I do. Lyric deserves more than the rare night out at a random bar and early morning orgasms. Although she does seem to really like the orgasms. Tonight, Lyric will get to experience one of my favorite places with all the bells and whistles.

Our driver parks near the back entrance of Aragon Ballroom, and the disappointment is obvious on Lyric's face. I want to chuckle, but I decide to play with her a little. "I just need to stop here for a second. Come with me."

She hesitates for a moment before sliding out of the seat and latching onto my hand. Rex hangs behind us, staying a safe distance back. He knows the plan and will ensure Lyric and I have our privacy.

As we walk, I imagine what it would be like to have her with me, just like this, every night. As my girlfriend and not my road manager. I'll never mention the fantasy to Lyric, though. Knowing how much she loves her job, it'll just piss her off. Instead, I keep it to myself and take her through the backstage hallway until we're turning down a dark and narrow passage.

We arrive at the stairwell leading to the roof when Lyric freezes in her tracks. We grind to a halt, and I turn toward her. She's probably creeped out.

I laugh and tug on her hand. "We're not here for work. I want to take you somewhere."

Her eyes aren't on me, though; they are fixed on a pocket of darkness beneath the stairs. I have a flashback to the first time I saw that little nook. The same night I stole the rooftop keys for the first time so that I could get away from it all. From my dad. The tour. His skanky bimbos. All of it.

After a moment, she turns to me and lets out an embarrassed laugh. "Sorry, I just remembered something. Where are you taking me?" she asks, curiously.

I wink. "To one of my all-time favorite places."

"So, this isn't a pit stop before our date?"

"This is our date, babe."

Her face doesn't give much away, so I lead her up the staircase, keeping a tight grip on her hand. The door is already unlocked, as planned. I open it and allow her to walk past me. When she does, she gasps. "Wolf," she breathes.

I had the entire rooftop decorated with strings of white twinkle lights and gas lanterns. Rose petals cover every surface, and a cloth-draped table sits in the center of it all with our dinner plates protected by silver domes. She looks around the space, taking it all in, her mouth wide in wonder. She's impressed.

Before she can say a word, I take her in my arms so the small of her back is pressed against me. "I thought we could have a private dinner with a view before the show." I run my nose from her cheek to the base of her neck, eliciting shivers all along her sexy body. The effect I have on her always makes me hard—even more than the thought of planting myself between her thighs.

"Come." I smirk, taking her hand again and pulling her toward the edge of the roof. I want her to understand why this is my favorite place. I want to tell her everything. I want to know everything about her. She already knows the important stuff about me. I'm hoping that maybe she'll let me in and talk about her parents. I won't pressure her. Never. But I want her to know it's okay if she does want to talk about anything.

We're a few feet from the edge of the roof when Lyric stops behind me. I can't explain the strange feeling I get in my chest, but it's almost as if we've done this before. Initially, I have a flashback to the first time I ever stepped foot onto the roof, tugging a scared girl behind me. And then Lyric's response to the dark corner beneath the stairs hits me like a sledgehammer.

No fucking way.

I turn to face her, my heart beating rapidly in my chest. "Lyric." I test her name to see if the same realization has hit her yet.

Her eyes flicker to mine. "Heights," she says, reminding me and confirming my suspicions all at once.

"Shit, babe, I thought it was just a sleeping on a bus thing," I say, feeling instantly like shit. But only a little bit, because I'm too distracted by my old memory.

And then I pull her into my arms, just like I did when I was fifteen, and—*holy shit*. I'm holding her close, but not like I usually do. I don't slam our bodies together and suffocate her mouth with mine. This time, I picture myself at fifteen, trying to comfort that scared girl who was petrified of heights.

"Lyric," I say again because there are no words for the coincidence we've just stumbled upon. I'm not even sure if she's connected the dots yet, but I sure as fuck remember. At fifteen, I had a raging boner for a girl I dragged up to the rooftop because she was sad. Her dad was sending her to live with her mom, and I wanted to make her feel better.

That girl was Lyric.

And the man who called her away from me was *Mitch fucking Cassidy*. If Mitch had been performing that night I might have made the connection, but he must have brought Lyric there to watch my dad's show.

"Beowulf," she says.

She remembers. *But wait.* I never told her my name. "What?"

"Beowulf," she repeats. "Some guy was calling out that name over and over after I left the rooftop with my dad. Is that your name?"

I nod. *Shit.* No one has called me that in years. "That was my dad." I look down at her again, still dazed by the coincidence. "This is insane," I finally say because I don't know what other words can describe what is happening now. I still think about that girl now and then. That girl who had to rush off like Cinderella at the stroke of midnight, except she didn't drop a thing. There was nothing left to remember her by—just my memories.

Lyric looks up at me. "Your dad was performing that night? That's how you got backstage."

I nod and swallow. "When he was with his old band. Before my mom got sick, I'd hang with him during my school breaks. He never paid me any attention, though. I hated touring with him."

"Which is why you escaped to the roof." She's grinning.

I brush my finger along her cheek. "And I heard you crying."

Her eyes close and she leans into my palm, releasing a sigh. "That fauxhawk was so sexy."

Her words throw me. She just lightened what could have been a very serious conversation.

I laugh. "I still style it like that sometimes."

She grins and slides two palms against the sides of my head. "I would love to see that. Do it for me?"

She has no clue that I would do *anything* for her. "I think that can be arranged." And then I have to ask. "What happened after you left to live with your mom?"

Lyric shrugs, trying to act nonchalant as Lyric does but failing this time. "*Destiny Lane* was busy. My mom was never there. I can count on two hands how many times I saw her before I graduated from high school and moved to Seattle."

"What? How is that possible? Who took care of you?"

"Deloris," Lyric responds sourly. "The nanny. Do you know how embarrassing it is to have a nanny when you're a teenager? Everyone thought Deloris was my mother, though. I guess it was easier that way since she was the one who picked me up from school and took me to the doctor's and stuff before I got my license." She rolls her eyes and then laughs. "Anyway, I thought about your fauxhawk for a long time after that night."

I chuckle. "I totally would have shoved my tongue down your throat if your dad hadn't interrupted us." When her face lights up, I lean in and touch her nose with mine. "I'm trying desperately hard not to shove my tongue down your throat right now, but it's our first date. I can't kiss you until it's over. And then I promise I won't stop kissing you until I have you against a wall. I just have to pick one."

I look up and pretend to have an internal debate about wall options. There are few to choose from and they all surround the rooftop door, but the debate is pointless. I've already chosen the one I want to see her convulse against.

Lyric slides her hands around my waist, links them together, and stares up into my eyes. "Deal."

Grinning and locking my arm in hers, I walk her to the table and hold out her chair. I sit across from her and lift my wine glass, gesturing for her to do the same. She does, and my chest swells when I see her wide smile. She's happy. I'm making her happy.

"To the first girl I ever snuck onto the rooftop of the Aragon."

She scoffs. "I hope you mean the only."

I laugh. "Yes, the only."

Our eyes lock as we sip from our glasses. When I set mine down I'm full of questions. Questions I can't believe I've never asked her before. Somehow along the way I went from wanting to one-night-stand Lyric to wanting to know everything about her. And I'm not even ashamed. "So tell me about Deloris. She still around?"

Lyric smiles, and I can already see the fondness she carries for the woman. "She's working for another family now. Destiny Lane let her go when I moved out." She laughs. "Let's just say Deloris is in a much better place. We're friends on social media, so I've seen the little girls she's looking over now, and I can see how much they adore her. It all worked out for the best."

I smile. I was fortunate enough not to have two parents in the industry. My mom was always there. Lyric didn't have that luxury. Thank God for Deloris.

"You should invite her to a show. I'm sure you'd love to see her again."

Lyric's eyes light up. "Really? Maybe if she can take some time off I could fly her out. She loves your music."

I catch the blush that creeps up her neck and into her cheeks. "Tell me more," I tease curiously.

She sighs and rolls her eyes. "I may have sent her your first CD when it came out. She was always supportive of my musical tastes, and I might have mentioned you to her a time or two." A deeper blush blossoms, and I think I'm enjoying this a little too much.

"Is that right?" I'm fully grinning now, and she leans back in embarrassment.

"Fine, confession," she says with her hands up. "I've always been a fan of your music. It's—I don't know—original. Healing too, in a way." She swallows.

Everything she's saying is exactly why I do this. I love that Lyric gets it. But she's always gotten it. Seen me through the music and the image. And in some strange way, I've always gotten her, too.

"Your album, *A Stranger Me*," she continues, "that was like, my life's soundtrack at the time it came out. I'd listen to it when I felt like I was losing myself, and it made me feel less alone."

She shrugs, and I can see so much in this moment. So much in her. All that she's lost and suffered. But most of all, how strong Lyric Cassidy truly is.

♪ ♪ ♪

We somehow manage to keep our hands off each other through dinner, but the moment we're done eating, I pull her to her feet and wrap my arms around her. "Dance with me," I say. Desire surges through me, and I know she can hear it in my voice—not that I'm trying to hide it. I want her. I always want Lyric, but tonight is different.

Tonight, Lyric's showing me a different side of her. One that isn't afraid to tell me she's been a fan of my music since the beginning. That, along the fact that we had a special bond when we were just fifteen years old, reaffirms that whatever is going on between us is not something I'll be letting go of anytime soon.

She returns my embrace, and we sway to the light rock music playing from the wireless speaker on our table. When she looks up at me with those beautiful green eyes, I get lost for moment. My lips find hers and I'm memorizing them, devouring them, until our bodies can't get any closer. I pick her up, and she wraps her legs around my waist. I palm her bare ass cheeks beneath her skirt and push my cock into her, but I'm blocked by too many layers of clothes. Lyric always wears the sexiest underwear, but right now, I just want to tear them off.

The chosen wall is a few feet away, so I walk her to it and place her back against it as promised. I always make good on my promises. She puts more of her sexy noises in my mouth, and I grind into her more eagerly than before.

"Can we just pretend I walked you home and gave you a sweet goodnight kiss? Because I really want to sink into your sweet pussy right now."

"Since you asked so nicely." Her lips curl up into a smile. "Hell yes."

I stand her up just to slip her panties from her and steal a taste along the line of wetness forming between her thighs. For a second, I consider throwing a leg over my shoulder and mouth-fucking her into oblivion, but this time, my need to be inside her is too great.

I quickly push my jeans and underwear down to my ankles. Then I effortlessly lift Lyric up, palming her ass again as she wraps her legs around me. I'd rather her be naked, but I won't risk it, knowing there's already a good chance we can be seen by neighboring windows. I press her backward so she's flush against the brick, my body protecting her from sight. If anyone is going to see anything, it'll be my ass, and I couldn't care less if anyone gets an eyeful of that.

My dick is already positioned perfectly to take her, although I still have to manage to put a condom on. Damn it.

"Wolf," she says, and I'm worried—worried that she wants to wait until we're in our hotel room in private. My dick flinches, as if readying itself for the rejection to follow. But when she speaks, she pants. "No mercy. Give it to me hard."

"Your wish is my command."

I snake a condom on as fast as physically possible and slide into her. With her back propped up against the wall, I support her head with one palm and her ass with the other.

Every stroke of my tongue in her mouth comes with a powerful thrust. And then I separate our mouths to look down. Her skirt hides my view so I maneuver it a little, folding it up into her waistband. And hell. There it is. I have to exercise massive self-control as I slow down my movements and watch every inch of my cock disappear inside her. My stomach muscles tighten as I pull out just as slowly as I entered. When I push back into her, she moans deeply. It's all too much.

Lifting my eyes from the show below, I take my hand from behind her head and unbutton her jacket, exposing her heaving breasts. Every bit of Lyric is so damn beautiful. I plant my face between her tits, close my eyes, and resume my powerful thrusts into her.

Usually I can control these situations. I can aim and shoot at my target with perfection, but not tonight. I'm inside her, but the build-up isn't under my control because I'm practically blinded by Lyric's insane beauty and sexual dominance. She's pinned against the wall, her arms are around my neck, and she's kissing me with as much abandon as I'm kissing her—but when she starts grinding, she weakens my thrusts. I let her have control.

I'm so attuned to Lyric's wants and needs; it goes against everything I've ever believed in when it comes to mixing sex and feelings. My badass rocker image is most definitely in question, but for Lyric, I'll make the sacrifice.

She tugs at my hair, and I send myself deeper into her until I'm seeing stars. She calls my name and I call hers back as my final thrusts bring us both unraveling into one another as the Chicago traffic blares below us.

Chapter Twenty

Lyric

We can't get enough of each other. For over a month, we lock ourselves in our rooms whenever we're not working and flirt blatantly when we are. It's not all about the sex, either, which is the most surprising part. We're writing together. Sometimes we're naked and teasing each other while we scribble in our notebooks, but we're productive about it. He's taken a few of the songs to the guys, and they get riled up each time. I can almost feel their itch to get back into the practice studio to hear how it all sounds.

And that's why I have a surprise for them.

We arrive at the Los Angeles venue earlier than usual this morning. The East Coast leg of the tour is over, and we're wrapping up the final few shows in California. As we near the venue, I catch a glimpse of familiar posters hanging from the surrounding fence. Salvation Road. Tony's band.

It doesn't bother me like it would have a month ago. In fact, it makes me giddy to know that loser didn't get the best of me. Wolf has all of me, good and bad, and it's so damn perfect. Ignoring the posters with Tony's face on them, I focus on the surprise I have in store for the guys.

I disregard the grumbles from the band and dodge Wolf's paws, which are clawing at me to come back to bed. "Who says you get to change the schedule on us? This is supposed to be morning sex time," he growls. "Look at this." He strokes his massive erection furiously.

I just laugh. "Not now, babe. Get up and meet us outside. I'll take care of you later."

He mutters something, but I'm already out the door and meeting Crawley at the bottom of the bus steps. He's the only one who knows what I've been up to. Somewhere along the way, he realized there was nothing he could do about the relationship brewing between Wolf and me, and although I know he's still pissed about it, he's backed off some. I'm still not even sure what to call this thing between us, but our attraction for each other is completely out in the open. It's hard to hide intense bus sex. Everyone's just happy we have a private room instead of a bunk.

Wolf is the last one off the bus. He's got a sour look on his face, but he approaches me anyway, moves around me, and wraps his arms around me from behind. "This better be worth the ice water I just had to toss on my dick."

My eyes go wide as I look back at him, and I just can't help it. I burst into laughter and spin around. Reaching up on my tiptoes, I kiss his nose and smile. "I promise it will be. Come."

He groans as I tug him toward the backstage entrance. "Don't remind me."

The guys follow us past security and out onto the open stage. The road crew is already setting everything up for us. I spread my arms wide and smile at the guys. "You have two hours of practice time. I've set it up at every venue from now until the end of the tour. No charge. It's up to you if you want to use it." Then I get a blast of insecurity. What if the last thing they want is to work before a huge show? Shit.

Hedge lets out a holler. "Fucking yes!"

Stryder picks me up and spins me around. "You're a mind reader, Lyric. We need this." He pats Wolf's shoulder in passing, and the rest of the band follow him to the stage. All but Wolf.

Wolf is staring at me, a new look in his eyes.

"You happy?" I ask him, hopeful.

There's a tug at his lips, and I know his response before he picks me up and wraps my legs around his waist.

"You're incredible, you know that?"

I tilt my head, unable to keep the smile from my face. "Well, if the rock star says so, it must be true."

He grins. "Damn straight. Give me those lips." He plants his mouth on mine and kisses me so hard it makes my head spin. I kiss him back, running my fingers through his unruly hair. I love the way I feel in Wolf's arms. Every single time we're together, he makes me feel this way. He shows me he's nothing like the rumors. Nothing like how he admits he used to be. He shows me I'm his and proves he's worthy to be mine.

I never want him to let me go. Not in this moment. Not ever.

It's a good few minutes into our make-out session before we hear Derrick calling to Wolf from the stage. He groans as he pulls away. "I'm going to fuck you crazy hard tonight. Get ready." He places me down on wobbly legs and runs to the stage with his famous wolf cry.

I haven't seen the guys have this much fun since our first nights out together. With the monotonous schedule they deal with on a daily basis, the excitement wanes, at least when they're on the stage. Listening to them collaborate on the instrumentals gives me my own high. Seeing Wolf smile in general lights up my world, but watching him laugh and be playful with the guys is like getting a heavy dose of endorphins shot straight into my veins.

♪ ♪ ♪

The show is the best the guys have done in a while, I think due to how relaxed they were all day. As much passion as they have for the music, there are times when it begins to feel like a job, and that's when the stress creeps in. There's so much energy radiating from them as they leave the stage; I know the rest of our evening consists of a club and copious amounts of alcohol.

Wolf is attached to my neck the entire way to the bar, whispering all the things he wants to do to me when we get back to the hotel. I'm quivering from his words by the time we get out of the car. His hand never leaves mine as we're pulled from a back entrance into the VIP lounge.

We order bottles for the table and rounds of shots to be delivered, then slam the first round back. As I set down my shot glass, Wolf pulls me onto his lap on the black leather couch. The room is awash in black lights, illuminating brightly colored chalkboard art and futuristic décor. Cigar smoke wafts through the air, and everything feels like it's vibrating as the DJ scratches and spins a techno beat.

Melanie bounces over a while later and pulls me to my feet. "Let's dance." She peers over my shoulder to a glaring Wolf. "Calm down, Wolfman. I'm borrowing your girl. I promise not to touch her naughty places."

He winks at her and puckers his lips at me. "Have fun."

Melanie leads me downstairs to the dance floor. Our bodies move to the beat, elation coming over me as the alcohol kicks in. I'm definitely buzzing. When an arm wraps around me from behind, I smile, surprised that Wolf decided to brave the crowd. Surely Crawley will not be okay with this. Neither will Rex.

When I catch Melanie's horrified expression, fear clenches tightly in my chest. I spin around to find a familiar face grinning down at me. It's not Wolf. The nearly black eyes staring back at me belong to the man who broke me. At least, I thought he did. It's completely clear to me now that he didn't, because he was never *the one*.

Tony Rain, lead singer of Salvation Road, whose new single has somehow managed to rank pretty damn near Wolf on the charts, is right in front of me.

"Hey, sweet pea." He's still smiling as if I didn't catch him fucking my best friend.

The blood begins to boil in my veins. "Get off me." I shove him away. "What are you doing here?" I'm fuming, but I decide I don't want to hear his answer and make a move to leave the dance floor.

"Sweet pea, stop." He rushes after me, yanking my arm and spinning me around.

Shit, that hurt. I rub my arm, glaring at him.

"Our show was last night, and we stayed to watch Wolf. I knew you were working his tour. I wanted to see you. Didn't you get my messages?"

Before I know what I'm doing, I throw my palm across his cheek. I wish I could hear the crack my hand makes against his skin, but the music is too loud. At least I can see the pain he suffers in response. "Get your hands off me." I turn and walk away.

"Lyric!" he roars, coming after me again. This time he grabs my neck through my hair, and I feel a small clump of hair tear away from my scalp. It stings and then burns. *What the hell?* He uses his hands as a vise to turn me so we're face-to-face. I don't move willingly. He's just stronger than me. And when Tony gets drunk, he loses his damn mind. But he's never hurt me before. Not physically, anyway.

"It's over. Between Joanna and me," he says with a familiar slur. "It's over." His breath, warm and scented with bourbon, sticks to my cheek. Chills run through me at the memory of constantly needing to take care for of Tony on nights he would drown himself in alcohol … and maybe some other stuff. I never knew for sure. I remember how frequent the incidents became, and how every time I'd have to remind Tony of what happened the night before.

He finally releases my neck.

"That's too fucking bad, Tony, because you two are meant for each other. Don't talk to me, don't touch me, don't message me, don't come near me. Get the fuck away." I shove him with both hands, but he only teeters a little.

I growl in frustration and turn to leave again. This time I hit a wall. Or rather, I collide with Wolf's chest. His eyes are on fire, and he's staring over my head at Tony.

Shit. No. This cannot be happening.

"She asked you to leave her alone."

Tony's laugh sends shivers racing up my spine. "If it isn't the big, bad Wolf. Please don't tell me you're fucking my woman. I will certainly kick your ass."

I look back at Tony, appalled at his audacity.

"You lost the right to talk to Lyric when you stuck your dick in some bimbo. Get out of here before I have you thrown out, you prick."

Tony throws back his shaved head and laughs again. Then he reaches for my elbow and leans in. "C'mon, sweet pea. Let's talk. I miss you, babe."

I can feel the heat raging beneath Wolf's shirt, and I look up, terrified of what I know is coming. It all happens in slow motion. Wolf shifts me to the side. Melanie stands there with an expression that registers disbelief. Her arms wrap around me, but she's focused on Wolf as he balls his hand into a fist.

"Oh shit," she says loud enough so that I can hear it. The club music is blaring, but as people around us notice Wolf and Tony standing inches apart, death stares on max intensity, a small crowd begins to form. Wolf is oblivious to everything but Tony. His lips curl, and then he cocks his arm back. Tony is so drunk he doesn't even know what's about to happen to him. He stands there, grinning, like he's not about to lose his teeth.

"I heard you loved pussy, but I never thought you'd lap up my seconds." Tony's tongue shoots out to lick his bottom lip while his eyes scroll my body. It's an obvious move to antagonize Wolf, and it works.

Wolf's fist shoots forward, connecting with Tony's cheek in a mean right hook. Blood sprays everywhere. Wolf steps forward, wrapping his thick fingers around Tony's neck and bringing his face in close. "Lyric's mine now, asshole. You hear that? You come near her again, I'll rip your tiny fucking dick off."

A wave ripples through the crowd as security pushes their way through. Rex gets to us first and pulls Wolf away. I step forward and wrap my arms around Wolf, my heart pounding wildly in my chest.

We watch as Rex grabs a stumbling Tony by the arms. When he's got him locked and ready to hand him over to security, he looks at Wolf, and nods toward the exit. "Go." His voice is as deep as the bass that bumps from the speakers, but we hear him loud and clear.

"Babe, let's go," I urge, squeezing his arm.

Wolf hesitates, his expression still set on kill mode, so I slip my hand into his and tug. "Wolf." My plea seems to break through to him this time and his eyes soften when he looks at me.

With a final look tossed in Tony's direction, he squeezes my hand. "Let's go."

I sigh with relief and we're moving toward the back entrance so fast, all I see are blurred faces as we pass.

Our driver is in the van on his phone when we exit the club. He sees us and puts it away as if he already knows we need to get the fuck out of here.

Wolf climbs in first and goes to the back of the van. He pulls me in, wrapping one arm around my shoulders and placing the other one on my upper thigh. His fingers dig in and his head falls into my hair, causing my pulse to quicken.

Neither of us speaks at first, and I know he's still riled up from the fight. But I think I'm more concerned about what Wolf might be thinking. I've never seen him act like that before. So … vicious.

My face falls when I see the swelling redness of his knuckles. "Baby, I am so sorry."

Wolf lifts his head, looking at me incredulously. "What? Why are *you* sorry? I went crazy cage fighter on your ex-boyfriend back there. Aren't you pissed at me?"

"No." Pressure starts to build in the back of my throat and a pinch of heat forms behind my eyes. "He's an asshole. He was an ass when we dated, but I didn't see it at first. By the time I started getting glimpses of who he really is, I didn't really care anymore."

"I can't believe you dated that prick. He fucking grabbed you by the neck, Lyric. Did he pull that shit when you were together?"

My eyes widen as they blur. "No. Never."

Wolf's eyes narrow. "But you loved him."

I shake my head without hesitation. "No." I cringe, knowing this is the time to lay it all out there. "I mean, we were together for two years." Wolf's expression dims, and I physically ache from his disappointment. I remove my seatbelt and crawl into his lap, straddle him, and use my palms to turn his face toward mine. We lock eyes and I pull in a big breath. "I couldn't have loved him. It's impossible…"

Fuck. Should I even say it?

"How is it impossible?" he asks, emotion building in his voice.

One deep breath later, I respond, "I didn't feel this way about him." I swallow. "The way I feel about you."

It happens in an instant. Wolf's chest expands, his eyes go soft, and his mouth captures mine. I mold to his body as his arms encase me tighter. And then he steals my breath, my heart, and my soul, all in one telling kiss. If there was any inkling of a question left whether pursuing something more with Wolf was right or wrong, this moment answers it.

When we finally part I have to fight against my nervous breathing to speak. "Wolf?" I ask, desperate to hear him say he feels the same.

"Not until we're in our room," he whispers in between kisses. "When I say it, I want to be inside you."

♪ ♪ ♪

Wolf is determined to make good on all his promises today.

He enters me, bare for the first time, thanks to my newly acquired birth control. His breath is heavy and staggered as he leans down to brush his lips against mine. A sweet kiss with a hint of playfulness that only promises dirty things to come.

One hand cups my head while the other lifts my leg, placing it over his shoulder. And then he presses against the back of my thigh as his girth sinks deeper.

My head is spinning through an endless, hazy cloud. I can feel all of him. Moving through me. Skin to skin. I've never gone bare before, and I can tell by the way that he's seated that he hasn't either. His lids squeeze shut and he breathes through his nose.

When he finally opens his eyes, they burn into mine with an intensity that should scare me, but I'm done being scared. I'm ready to love.

"I love you," he says while my fingers rake through his hair. My throat tightens and my eyes water. He smiles. "So fucking much it makes my heart hurt and my head spin. But if this ache in my chest comes from loving you, then I'll take it."

And then he begins to move.

Those words and the fullness of him rocking into me makes my entire body tingle. Everything is sensitive.

"I want this," he says each word in between each thrust. "I want us." Then he leans in and kisses my ear before dragging his nose down the side of my neck and speaking softly. "Jesus, say something." He chuckles air.

I cup his chin, brushing against his cheek with my thumb, my other hand digging into his neck. "I want us too," I promise. "I love you too." I smile. "So fucking much."

He groans, his movements more powerful with each thrust. Each one makes my heart race a little faster and my toes curl a little more. I'm taking all of him, feeling his naked flesh plunge and slide against mine. It's the most incredible feeling in the world. And now I know this is what he meant when he promised to fuck me crazy-hard. Wolf doesn't lie.

The hint of another orgasm simmers through me, a slight buzz at first, but then the intensity grows. He feels it. He gives me that knowing smile before flipping me onto my chest. In one quick motion, he lifts my hips and enters me again, not wasting a second. The buzz takes me to the edge, and I'm only moments away from spiraling out of control.

"Wolf," I warn, pleading with him over my shoulder.

His eyes shoot to mine like a rabid dog in the wild, finding his long-awaited prey. His face lights up and he leans over my back, sliding one hand around until it's on my clit.

"Come, baby. All over my cock." He kisses my back. "You can do it."

I tremble at his words. The sensation shoots from my core like a starburst, reaching every tip of my body.

"Good girl," he coos in my ear, then nips at my shoulder. "You ready for me?"

I nod, distracted as I ride out my release.

He maneuvers me so that I'm facing him again without ever pulling out. Then he leans forward, taking my mouth in his.

On his last thrust before he empties his everything into me, he looks me in the eyes. "I fucking love you, baby."

My hand goes to his heart, wanting to feel every beat as he fills me.

"I fucking love you too."

Chapter Twenty-One

Wolf

I once was a man who feared repeat sexual encounters. And then Lyric Cassidy walked into my life. Now I'm a man all too willing to open an on-demand orgasm factory for his girlfriend.

Like my music, she's become my craving. My obsession. I can't get enough. So when that douchebag, Tony, showed up at the club and put his unwelcome paws on her, I had to stake my claim. Lyric is mine, and I want to be hers. There's simply no one else that can satisfy my needs because she created them, and there's nothing I want more than to protect her from any more heartbreak. She deserves the world, and I want to give it to her.

Last night in the car, I was fuming. Not just because I all but punched a hole through Tony's face, but because Lyric was once wrapped up in a relationship with him. What was she thinking? He's a no-good punk. To be honest, for a second I wondered if she fell for me for the same reasons. Bad boy rocker with an ugly ego. I'm all those things, too, but after just one taste of Lyric, I couldn't imagine fucking her over. Ever.

And then she told me she loved me. I could hear the words on her breath before she spoke them, and I probed her, wanting to hear her say it. I've never wanted to hear those words from a woman before. But the moment I thought the words might slip from Lyric's lips, there was nothing I wanted more.

This morning, I'm drinking her in. The sunlight streaming through the window shines on her where she lies wrapped in the sheets, looking like an angel. My angel. She stirs slightly. I know that stir. She's waking up, but she's too comfortable to open her eyes.

I'm about to crawl under the covers to give her something pleasant to lift the morning fog when someone pounds on the door.

Bang! Bang! Bang!

What the fuck? The urge to rip someone's head off for startling Lyric overcomes me. The pounding starts again before I can jump out of bed. There's a muffled voice on the other side. "God dammit, open the goddamn door!"

The unsolicited disturbance is Crawley. I grab my shorts and try not to trip putting them on as I shuffle to the door. I look back at Lyric, who seems to be getting more uncomfortable by the second. She rolls over and pulls a pillow over her head. I yank the door open, but only a few inches.

"What the hell do you want? Lyric's still sleeping."

Crawley's face says it all. He's pissed, and it only takes me two seconds to guess why. He shoves his phone in at me. Tony's bloodied face stares back at me. I look away.

"We have a problem on our hands, Chapman. Your girlfriend seems to be causing more trouble than she's worth. She's going to cost you this tour if you're not careful."

Ignoring the phone, I step in the hallway. I narrow my eyes and get right into Crawley's face. We're the same height and size, so he doesn't back down, but he needs to remember who tells who what to do around here. "Watch your mouth, Crawley. I have no problem tossing your ass if you keep up this shit. Lyric isn't causing problems. You, on the other hand—"

Crawley shakes his head, cutting me off. His face turns beet red. "You're not listening to me. I care about your career, Wolf, because it's my career, too. And right now, you've got your dick in la la land. You need to eject yourself, no pun intended, from whatever this is before it blows up in your face." He shoves his phone at me again, showing me there's more than the one photo. "We've got a PR nightmare on our hands. Get dressed and let's go deal with this shit. Leave your *girlfriend* here."

The picture that lights up on Crawley's phone now is a classic photo of my Hulk face just as my fist made impact with Tony's cheek. It's a badass picture. You can even see the trail of spit as it leaves Tony's mouth.

Crawley slides his finger across the screen so I can see the next photo. One by one, the pictures tell a story of how I messed up Tony's face over a woman. And the headlines are worse. Somehow, in my effort to protect Lyric from her asshole ex-boyfriend, I became a madman who tried to steal Tony's girlfriend and then beat him to a bloody pump. *Tony's girlfriend.*

"These stories are shit. None of this is true. Tony was hurting Lyric. You should have seen the way he grabbed her, Crawley. I was protecting my girl."

Crawley yanks his phone back and shoves it in his back pocket. "Look, I don't care if you revealed yourself as Batman and saved the fucking planet last night. We've got to get on the phone with PR and get us a story quick. And the tour company wants to speak with Lyric."

Anger radiates through me as I stare back at Crawley. "Why?"

"She's off the tour. We can't afford to have her mess this up for us."

I glare at him. "She's not leaving. Your ass is going home before she does. I mean it. You've been with us for as long as we've been around, but I don't give a shit what anyone says. This is my tour, and she's staying."

"They'll fire her if she stays. It's not my call. The articles aren't just about you, Wolf. They're about her, too."

"I don't give a fuck about the articles," I yell. "None of it's true. You can't just fire someone because the tabloids and paparazzi made shit up. This is my tour. When the fuck did you start thinking you could trump my decisions?"

Crawley taps his finger on my chest, and I'm seconds away from latching on and breaking it. Who the hell does he think he is? "You pay me to make these decisions. You may have forgotten that, but I'm doing what you hired me to do. I have a stake in all of this, too, and you better believe I'll watch out for what's mine.

"You wanted me to protect the girl's secret? Well, those lyrics may be legally yours now, but that doesn't mean we can't leak who signed them over to us. That small detail was left out of the contract, and Lyric obviously has something to hide. Unless you both want that secret exposed, I suggest you start following my lead."

I ball my fists at my sides. Prick. "Are you blackmailing me, Crawley?"

235

"No." He shakes his head and laughs. "But I am blackmailing your girlfriend. You won't need to do a thing."

With that, Crawley turns to walk away. Rage fills my chest. "Don't think I won't have your ass tossed for this, dickhead!" I don't care who the fuck hears me.

Crawley turns to face me, but he keeps walking. "I think you're smarter than that. Six years gives me a lot of shit to unleash if you decide to do anything stupid." I'm racking my brain for anything he could possibly have on me. I'm coming up empty, but I'm not in the right state of mind to be making these decisions. All I see is red.

"Say goodbye to your lady friend," Crawley calls like a madman, a mega-watt smile on his face. "She goes home today. And you should probably start checking your messages. You have a long day ahead of you." He disappears into the next elevator.

I'm trying to control my breathing when the door to the room opens and Lyric's sleepy head pops out, followed by the rest of her body. Her hair is messy, and she's wearing a white tank top and shorts. Her nipples are at full attention, but for the first time since meeting her, I don't want to rip off her clothes and make her moan. I want to hold her as tight as I can until I figure out how I'm going to make this right.

"Babe?" she asks. The worry in her expression kills me.

I step forward and nudge her into the room before closing the door and locking it behind us. I lean against it and squeeze my eyes shut, trying to calm down before I open my mouth. Her arms snake around my waist, and she nuzzles my chest. I'm sugar in her hot glass of water—I totally dissolve into her the moment we touch. But even though she's right fucking here, I feel as if she's slipping from me. It was only a matter of time.

"Wolf, you're scaring me."

I grip her face with my palms and look into her eyes. "I love you, Lyric. You know that, right?"

She nods without a sliver of hesitation, and my heart wants to explode. "I love you, too. What's going on? Is it because of Tony?"

"Have you checked your phone?"

She shakes her head as much as my hold will allow. I'm not ready to let her go. "No, why?"

"That was Crawley. He says we're in a deep pile of shit. Both of us. There are pictures all over the internet and articles spreading lies. Because of Tony. And your company wants you off the tour."

Her eyes widen and then narrow. "No."

At first I think she's saying no, she's not leaving the tour, and hope balloons in my chest, but then she pulls away and practically runs to her phone, and I'm deflated. As she scans her messages, I decide to do the same. There are literally thousands of missed calls, emails, and social media notifications. All in the span of less than twelve hours. I'm overwhelmed, and I haven't even opened a single one.

"Oh my God," Lyric breathes.

I go to her because I'm honestly more concerned for her fate than mine. "What?"

She's staring open-mouthed at her phone as she continues to read. "They're sending Doug to take over the tour, and they're sending me a car. Shit. Wolf, how the hell did this happen?"

"We didn't do anything wrong. There is absolutely nothing in our contracts that state anything about a relationship, not that it should fucking matter, anyway. This is my tour. My life. And if I want to fuck my road manager, I will." I'm so pissed, and I know the words I'm spewing aren't kind. "It's Crawley. All fucking Crawley. I wouldn't be surprised if he was the one who took the pictures and leaked them."

Lyric looks at me, and her eyes are full of doubt and wishful thinking. "No. I know he's a prick, but why would he want to hurt us like that? He's ecstatic about the songs."

With a sigh, I bow my head. "That's the other thing. Crawley says if you don't leave, he'll make sure everyone knows the songs are yours."

Lyric's eyes go wide, and she jumps up. "He can't do that! I signed those songs over to you. You, Crawley, and the lawyers are the only ones who know."

"He said that there was no agreement to keep your involvement with the songs a secret. But that's the only hold he has on us, babe. Who cares if people know you wrote them? You still signed them over. It's not like you'll be flooded with fame and fortune because of it."

Her expression falls, and for a moment she looks like she might cry, but instead, she hardens and turns to me. "It's completely out of the question. No one can know about the lyrics, Wolf. That was the deal when this all started."

Now I'm starting to get pissed. How can she let some silly song lyrics keep us apart? "You'd rather leave the tour than let people know you wrote some songs? Lyric, you have to know how ridiculous that sounds."

"Ridiculous?" She's fuming. "You think my secrets are ridiculous? If you remember correctly, you stole my secrets, and now I'm getting kicked off a tour because of what you took from me."

"What?" I don't believe what I'm hearing. She's pissed at *me?* Is she even listening to herself? "You mean the secrets you tossed in the trash? Meant that much to you, huh?"

I don't know why I'm provoking her, or why we're arguing about the lyrics. We're both insanely heated and borderline irrational. We agreed in the beginning it would all be a secret, and I fully intended to respect her wishes. But the thought of her leaving absolutely crushes me. Everything we've built together is about to blow up in our faces, and there's nothing I can do to stop it.

Without another word, Lyric grabs her overnight bag and begins packing. "What are you doing?" I roar. She can't leave me.

"What do you think?" She doesn't even look at me.

"Babe, stop." I reach for her, but she slaps my hand away.

"I need to pack."

I sink onto the bed, my chest tightening. I watch as Lyric flies around the room, gathering her things and shoving them into her bag. I'm racking my brain for anything I can say or do to help this messed up situation. When it looks like she's gathered everything, she pauses, and I think she might stop and say something to me. But when she turns and walks away instead, I shake off my fog and reach for the door before she can open it. My hands shoot out, slamming against the door and caging her in as she swivels to face me. Her eyes spit fire.

"Is that what I deserve? You're going to walk out the door without so much as a goodbye?"

I haven't seen Lyric this angry since the night she walked in on Jenn and me. Just that thought weakens me.

"Goodbye, Wolf," she says, but it's not as cold as her expression is. I hear her voice crack. I know she's just reacting to the situation. This can't be a reflection of our time together. Our connection.

"You don't need to leave." I'm pleading now. "We can figure this out together."

Lyric turns away. "It doesn't sound like I have a choice. It's either you or my *ridiculous* secrets. I think I'll keep my secrets, thank you very much."

Her words hurt like hell, but they're also revealing. There's something she's not telling me. Before, when she was upset about people knowing she wrote those songs, it seemed like she just didn't want the attention. Now, I think her reasons run deeper than that, and I'll be damned if I don't get to the bottom of it.

"I'm going to talk to Crawley. I'll toss him if I have to. I don't trust him after this. If you want to leave and work things out at the office, then go. I'll fix the PR mess, and then you can come back. If you can't come back as my road manager, then maybe you can take a break and travel with me."

Her eyes narrow. "You mean be your groupie?"

"No, Lyric. Fuck." Why is she talking like this? "I mean be my girlfriend. Work doesn't have to get in the way anymore. I just want you here with me."

"And what about *my* job, Wolf? I can't just give up my life because I met a hot rock star with a new outlook on life.

This was never supposed to be anything more than a one-time hookup, and you know it. We took it too far, and now look at us."

I didn't realize Lyric could turn her ferocity on me like this. But there she goes. Her words are her weapons, and I've lost count of how many times she's stabbed me. All I know is that it fucking hurts.

I move away from her and hold my hands up, not liking the way this is ending one bit, but I won't let anyone speak to me like that. "You know what? You go take care of you. Keep your lyrics locked away. Do whatever you need, but don't you dare play the victim card here. I'm asking you to stay. To be with me. To figure this out *with me*. If that's not what you want, too, then get the fuck out."

Her gasp is the last thing I hear before the door opens and slams shut behind her, effectively shredding my heart.

Fuck love.

Never a-fucking-gain.

Chapter Twenty-Two

Lyric

Doug meets me in the hotel lobby with a sympathetic look. If anyone gets life on the road and mixing business with pleasure, it's him. He's one of the most successful tour directors in the business, and he's not only married to one of his ex-clients, he's gay. He knows how the business can chew you up and spit you out. And he can see that I've been gnawed on. Still, his sympathy doesn't help my situation. I've read through about a dozen entertainment news articles shared all over social media about my infidelity to Tony. *My* infidelity. It makes me sick.

Doug immediately wraps his arms around me, and it warms my heart. I'm not surprised by his affection. He has always been fatherly toward me, and at times like this, the comfort is appreciated. "Let's go grab a drink."

I laugh and wipe a tear from my eye. "It's nine in the morning."

He winks. "As good a time as any. Come. We only have an hour."

He leads me to the hotel bar and orders us bloody mimosas and a fruit platter before turning to me with a sigh. "How are you holding up?"

I shrug. "I woke up to a million messages telling me I'm an asshole for cheating on Tony with Wolf and that I'm off the tour. Doug, the media can say whatever they want about me. I don't care. But they should know that Tony and I have been over for a while now. And Wolf—I think I really messed things up with him. My career, too." I bury my face in my hands. "If this is the end of my career, I don't know what I'm going to do."

"Are you and Wolf really a thing?"

His question doesn't shock me like it should. I guess I'll be asked this a lot. I nod. "It shocked me too, trust me."

"That's new for Wolf, but I'm not surprised he fell for you." I want to smile at the compliment, but my heart still hurts. "I guess you knew it wasn't going to last with the way his reputation precedes him."

I can't agree with Doug on this one. I've gotten to know Wolf pretty damn well, and he's done nothing but prove everyone wrong. He's never once hurt me—not until today, when he called my secrets ridiculous. I know it wasn't his intention to hurt me, and in his defense, I haven't exactly confessed my reasons for keeping my lyrics private. I wasn't ready to go there. Even after he told me about his parents ... it just wasn't the right time.

"I don't believe rumors anymore."

"Really?" Doug asks, but I can tell he's reading in between the lines. "Okay, then, care to tell me who the mystery songwriter is? This 'Dangerous Heart' song is a sensation, and it hasn't even been recorded yet."

My face heats. Doug is one of the few people who knows about my songs. "It's a mystery for a reason."

He sucks in a breath. "Holy shit, Lyric. I was right. Your dad would be so proud."

"The point of the mystery," I say dryly.

He sighs. "Lyric, you've got to let it go, don't you think? This grudge you're holding against your parents. It's only hurting you. Maybe they deserve to suffer for everything they've put you through, but you deserve to be happy."

"I *was* happy until Tony showed up and I got kicked off the tour."

"This isn't about one tour. This is about your life and understanding your self-worth. You had a unique situation growing up; it wasn't the best—I get that. But you've done pretty damn well for yourself despite it all, and that's something to be proud of. But you're holding yourself back. Settling on these one-off road jobs for what? To get away from your problems? They're never going to go away if you don't face them. Why don't you take this time for yourself? Deal with the heavy shit and then come back?"

"Come back on tour?"

He shrugs. "Maybe after you deal with all of this, you'll have a better idea of what you want for yourself. I can tell you one thing: suppressing your songwriting is a mistake. A huge mistake."

"I'm not suppressing it," I say. "I'm just hiding it. I don't need that kind of attention on myself."

Doug groans. "Hiding it is suppressing it. Writing for yourself may be healing, but that kind of talent should be shared with the world. Shit, Lyric. You don't see it, do you? What you can do with words?"

"You sound like my father. Doug, really. I get what you're doing, but right now, all I can think about is what the fuck I'm going to do once I leave this tour." *And how much I'm going to miss Wolf.*

Doug's hand reaches the back of my neck and squeezes. "Okay. I'll let up on you. Just go talk to the executives. I don't think your career is over unless you want it to be. I was only trying to convince you that maybe this was all for the best. Sometimes you need hurdles in life, the kind that come out of nowhere and make you stumble. Because when you get back up, you have a chance to dust yourself off and change direction. But it's your life, and the path you follow is your choice to make."

♪ ♪ ♪

My car is waiting for me when Doug and I finish breakfast. I'm buzzing from the alcohol, which is probably a good thing because I see the tour buses pulled up to the side of the hotel. The band and crew are already boarding. I try not to pay attention to who is getting on, afraid to make eye contact with one person in particular. And then a warm body brushes past me, and my heart stops. I know it's Wolf by the smell of his aftershave and the electricity that moves with him. When he continues walking by without a word to me, my heart cracks a little. I know the silence is my doing. This time, I have no one to blame but myself.

I want to reach out to him, to run after him when he nears bus number one. I want to jump on it with him and say to hell with my career, but my feet feel like lead. He deserves an apology, at least. An explanation. He deserves so much more than I'm giving him right now. I know that getting in the company car without talking to him could be the absolute end of any communication between us from here on out. My throat constricts at the thought. My chest is heavy, making breathing the most difficult fucking thing in the world.

"Do you want to say goodbye?" Doug asks.

I take a step toward Wolf, my eyes never leaving his back, even when he disappears onto the bus. My eyes follow the faint outline of his body as he walks straight down the narrow passageway toward his room. And then I stop myself and swallow, knowing there's too much damage to undo. There are no promises that can possibly make anything better.

I shake my head and face Doug, running a finger below my eye to catch a falling teardrop. "Oh, sweetie." He pulls me in and holds me for a minute, but it only makes the tears fall harder. "I'll call you in a few days. Everything will be okay."

With a final nod, I wipe my tears with the back of my hand, push my shoulders back, and slide into the backseat of the car. My eyes return to the windows of the bus, hoping to catch another glimpse of Wolf. At this point it's hard to make anything out through the tinted windows, but I know he's there. I know he's already shredding every last thought of me, because while I came on this tour to run from one dangerous heart, I smacked right into another … or so I thought.

Come to find out, the only dangerous heart around here belongs to me.

Next in the A Stolen Melody Duet
AVAILABLE SUMMER 2017

*Until the very end…
whenever that may be*

destined hearts

A STOLEN MELODY DUET #2

K.K. ALLEN

He stole her lyrics, and then he stole her heart.

Lyric Cassidy is off the tour, lost as to what her next career move will be, and certain that she'll never love again after Wolf. All because of a social media scandal that left her with no choice but to pack up and face the consequences. When she learns that the fate of her career is in her hands, she has a difficult decision to make. Step back on the tour bus with Wolf and deal with the mess she left behind, or end her contract early and lose her job at Perform Live?

Wolf's shattered heart finds no resolve in giving Lyric a chance to come back on tour. He can never be with her again. Not after she walked away. Conflicted with wants and needs, he struggles to remember who Wolf was before Lyric. That's what he needs to become again. Maybe then his heart will be safe. Or maybe there's no hope for the damaged.

But with stolen dreams, betrayals, and terrifying threats—no one's heart is safe. Not even the ones that may be destined to be together.

#

For new release announcements, **add Destined Hearts to your** *Goodreads TBR and follow K.K. on social media.*

Want More?

You do not want to miss what K.K. is working on next ;)
Sign up for new release alerts to never miss a thing!

SIGN UP HERE
smarturl.it/KK_MailList

Thank You

First, thank you to my readers! I know this novel is a bit different from other books of mine, but I hope you enjoyed it just the same. You'll never find a magic formula to my creations, so you can never expect the same thing twice. And special thanks to those of you reading this novel for the second time! I hope you find this new and enhanced version everything it's meant to be and more!

This duet was inspired by a time in my life when music was my everything. When I worked for a popular radio station and the rock star sightings were endless, the concerts were free, and my CD collection was bigger than my book collection. I was spoiled by great people and great music.

So, thank you KISS 106.1 in Seattle for providing me years of inspiration, industry insight, and eye candy to write these novels. Some of the best times of my life were spent walking your halls, answering phones in the studio for Marcus D, videotaping live concerts, rocking the club nights with DJ Tamm, tattooing strangers at the Puyallup Fair, and cruising around in the KISS van.

Thank you Roxie, Jennifer, Joy, Stephanie, and Anonymous (LOL) for your Beta reading skills. I appreciate the time you put into this one and all the feedback given to make Wolf and Lyric's story perfect.

Roxie and Jen, thank you for encouraging me to pull this book from the darkness. Without you two this story would have floated to the bottomless pit of Amazon, but you were right there to help reel Lyric and Wolf in, and help breathe life into their story.

Shauna Ward, you know I love you. Thank you for your eagerness to read something completely different from what you're used to getting from me, and for helping me maintain my voice while reshaping this story. I always say it, but it's true, you are so much more than an editor and I couldn't have done this without you.

Dylan Allen! Thank you for being the first one to read this and for supporting my work like crazyballs. Can't wait to see where your career takes you!

Foreword PR & Marketing, especially my publicist, Linda. Thank you, doll face! I love you and have so much respect for you and all that we've accomplished together since we started working together. You truly make my heart (and calendar) full.

Mom, I'm sorry I wouldn't let you read this one. If you happen to pick it up and read it … I'm sorry. #NotReally. I love you.

Eric David Battershell, I adore you! Thank you for introducing me to Johnny Kane and being one of the sweetest humans I've ever met. To Johnny Kane. I still can't find that damn story you tagged me in on Instagram! These are the things that drive me bonkers.

Sarah Hansen with Okay Creations, thank you for another beautiful cover! I love working with you, doll.

To Kristy Love. Thank you for pulling me out of blurb-writing hell. I probably owe you my life. Ha!

Thank you Gel Ytayz and InBookEden for the beautiful teasers! Can't wait to see that tattoo <3

Ashleigh, thanks again for your crazy passion for my work and for always being there to support my creations and me! Love you, girl.

To my Forevers!!! I love you to the ends of the Earth, the moon and back, and all that jazz. You are so special to me. You give me the best place to spend my days and you never let me forget why I work 18 hour days to get you stories to read.

Much Love,

K.K. Allen
XXOO

Let's Connect

Dear Reader, I hope you enjoyed Part One of Lyric and Wolf's story! If you have a few minutes to spare, please consider leaving a review on Amazon and Goodreads. Reviews mean the world to an author. You can also connect with me on social media and sign up for my mail list to be sure and never miss a new release, event, or sale!

K.K.'s Website & Blog: www.KK-Allen.com
Facebook: www.Facebook.com/AuthorKKAllen
Goodreads: www.goodreads.com/KKAllen
Twitter: www.Twitter/KKAllenAuthor

Join

JOIN K.K.'S INSIDERS GROUP, FOREVER YOUNG!

Enjoy special sneak peeks, participate in exclusive giveaways, enter to win ARCs, and chat it up with K.K. and special guests ;)

JOIN US HERE

www.facebook.com/groups/foreveryoungwithkk

Books
by K.K. Allen

Sweet & Inspirational Contemporary Romance
Up in the Treehouse
Under the Bleachers

Sweet & Sexy Contemporary Romance
Dangerous Hearts
Destined Hearts

Young Adult Fantasy
The Summer Solstice Enchanted
The Equinox
The Descendants

Short Stories and Anthologies
Soaring
Echoes of Winter

Up in the Treehouse (Chloe and Gavin's Story)

Up in the Treehouse (Chloe and Gavin's Story)

I wanted to tell him all my secrets, but he became one of them instead.

Chloe Rivers never thought she would keep secrets from her best friend. Then again, she never imagined she would fall in love with him either. When she finally reveals her feelings, rejection shatters her, rendering her vulnerable and sending her straight into the destructive arms of the wrong guy.

Gavin Rhodes never saw the betrayal coming. It crushes him. Chloe has always been his forbidden fantasy—sweet, tempting, and beautiful. But when the opportunity finally presents itself, he makes the biggest mistake of all and denies her.

Now it's too late …

Four years after a devastating tragedy, Chloe and Gavin's world's collide and they find their lives entangling once again. Haunted by the past, they are forced to come to terms with all that has transpired to find the peace they deserve. Except they can't seem to get near each other without combatting an intense emotional connection that brings them right back to where it all started … their childhood treehouse.

Chloe still holds her secrets close, but this time she isn't the only one with something to hide. Can their deep-rooted connection survive the destruction of innocence?

Under the Bleachers (Monica & Zach's Story)

Under the Bleachers (Monica & Zach's Story)

One kiss can change everything.

Fun and flirty Monica Stevens lives for chocolate, fashion, and boys ... in that order. And she doesn't take life too seriously, especially when it comes to dating. When a night of innocent banter with Seattle's hottest NFL quarterback turns passionate, she fears that everything she once managed to protect will soon be destroyed.

Seattle's most eligible bachelor, Zachary Ryan, is a workaholic by nature, an undercover entrepreneur, and passionate about the organizations he supports. He's also addicted to Monica, the curvy brunette with a sassy mouth—and not just because she tastes like strawberries and chocolate. She's as challenging as she is decadent, as witty as she is charming, and she's the perfect distraction from the daily grind.

While Monica comes to a crossroads in her life, Zachary becomes an unavoidable obstacle, forcing her to stop hiding under the bleachers and confront the demons of her past. But as their connection grows stronger, she knows it only brings them closer to their end.

It's time to let go.

To have a future, we must first deal with our pasts. But what if the two are connected?

The Summer Solstice Series

A Young Adult Fantasy series, appropriate for all ages.

The Summer Solstice Series is a Contemporary Fantasy / Romance series inspired by magic, nature, and love. Rich with Greek mythology, romance, and friendship, the community of Apollo Beach is threatened by something dark ... someone deadly.

About the Author

K.K. Allen is an award-winning author and Interdisciplinary Arts and Sciences graduate from the University of Washington who writes Contemporary Romance and Fantasy stories about "Capturing the Edge of Romance." K.K. currently resides in central Florida, works full time as a Digital Producer for a leading online educational institution, and is the mother to a ridiculously handsome little dude who owns her heart.

K.K.'s multi-genre publishing journey began in June 2014 with the YA Contemporary Fantasy trilogy, *The Summer Solstice*. In 2016, K.K. published her first Contemporary Romance, *Up in the Treehouse*, which went onto win the Romantic Times 2016 Reviewers' Choice Award for Best New Adult Book of the Year. With K.K.'s love for inspirational and coming of age stories involving heartfelt narratives and honest characters, you can be assured to always be surprised by what K.K. releases next.

More works in progress will be announced soon. Stay tuned for more by connecting with K.K. in all the social media spaces.

www.KK-Allen.com

Made in the USA
San Bernardino, CA
21 June 2017